Gerard Brady grew up in Dublin. He now teaches English in Lancashire. He and the author were married in 1971.

Ruth Carr is editor of The Female Line *and author of the contemporary women's fiction section of the* Field Day Anthology of Irish Literature.

'An Irish fairytale' and 'The last thing' first appeared in The Female Line *(Belfast, 1985). 'Women are the scourge of the earth' first appeared in* Wildish Things *(Dublin, 1989). None of the other stories have previously been published.*

WOMEN
– ARE THE –
SCOURGE
OF THE EARTH

Frances Molloy

The White Row Press

WOMEN
– ARE THE –
SCOURGE
OF THE EARTH

Frances Molloy

The White Row Press

First published 1998
by the White Row Press
135 Cumberland Road, Dundonald
Belfast BT16 OBB

This book has received financial assistance from
the Arts Council of Northern Ireland

Cover: detail from Hunter's Moon, requiem for Bela Bartok,
by Colin Middleton, reproduced with the kind permission of
Mrs Kate Middleton, and the Arts Council of Northern Ireland.

Cover: Nick Scott.
Typesetting: Island Publications
Printed by the Guernsey Press

A catalogue record for this book is available from the British Library

ISBN 1 870132 90 4

Contents

For Michael

Monster:	*'Oh Frankenstein... remember that I am thy creature; I ought to be thy Adam, but I am rather the fallen angel, whom thou drivest from joy for no misdeed. Everywhere I see bliss, from which I alone am irrevocably excluded. I was benevolent and good; misery made me a fiend. Make me happy, and I shall again be virtuous.*
Frankenstein:	*Be gone. I will not hear you. There can be no community between you and me, we are enemies.*

Frankenstein *Mary Shelley*

About the author

I met Frances in 1970 in Dublin, at Croke Park, at an All-Ireland semi-final in which Derry were involved. I remember nothing else about this time except being infatuated with this funny, joyful woman. I knew she was older than me. I was eighteen, she was twenty-three, but looked about sixteen. I lied to her about my age in case I got the big push. She told me later when the truth came out I would have done, but by then the die was cast. Our lives were inextricably linked together.

In those days I had ambitions to write. She, I think, was taken in and impressed by this. She encouraged me. She was always asking me to write stories for her, usually some variation of 'The devil's gift'. I found difficulty empathising with a sixteen year old nun. She was very persistent. When I eventually decided to try something else she took on the writer's mantle.

We went to England for a year, where we got married. Our daughter was born there. In 1971 we moved back to Northern Ireland. We lived there for two years in County Derry. Our son was born there. The Troubles showed no respite. Frances worried about me, a Dubliner, living in the north. She also did not want her children growing up in a bitter sectarian environment. I loved the warmth and support of the extended family I did not have. I left reluctantly. She, after any length of time, found it oppressive and claustrophobic. She wanted to start again and we came back to England where we had friends.

The seventies were the happiest years of her life. The house was always full of children. She enjoyed storytelling and loved an audience. She inherited this gift from both her parents.

In 1980 she began to write some sketches and stories for a couple of writing circles in the Lancaster area. They were well received. This gave her confidence. She was torn between the desire to write and receive a full time education. At that time I was a mature student at Lancaster University. She supported me. The plan was that I would do the same for her when I got my degree. Meantime she ran a household and wrote. And then, quite unexpectedly, success. Writing took on a life of its own for five years.

Frances hated her work being pigeon-holed. She was wary of literary ideology. She believed that her only purpose in writing was to write about the people she described as 'her characters'. They are nearly all damaged and weak. They battle for survival in a hostile world. 'Society's rejects' she called them. She had no doubt that she was one. She used dialect, not to indicate any comical oddity in the people she was writing about, but rather as an aid to write about people and events which she felt were ignored. Despite her poor formal education she quickly became a very skilled and sophisticated reader, with an acute critical intelligence.

No Mate for the Magpie's success was a shock. She worried about her family's and friends' reaction to its depiction of real and imaginary events. She hated being asked if it was an autobiography, or if all the events depicted had actually happened. She described it as a kind of embroidered autobiography which she felt was psychologically true.

Her writing was becoming more accomplished. She wanted to develop more balance. She experimented with omniscient narrators, and more orthodox prose. But dissatisfied, she turned again to first person narrators. She didn't enjoy the shade and depth she felt compelled to give her characters. She was conscious of a criticism that she did not use her stories to openly challenge and attack hypocrisy. She would argue that the resignation of some of her characters was not a condoning of stereotypes, but rather a truthful reflection of the society she knew.

She often said she could only write about Ireland, in England. Ireland was a kind of force that inhibited and neutralised her creative imagination. She needed distance to write with detachment and irony.

In 1990 Frances enrolled as a mature student at the University of Central Lancashire. She was taking a break from writing, she said. Whereas she had felt compelled to write the stories, this was something she was doing for herself. She was a complex person. She had a great capacity for friendship and kindness, for her the greatest virtue. And yet she could be the most demanding and infuriating person on God's earth. She would ask for advice, 'Don't spare me, be truthful.' But if it was less than laudatory, look out. Yet invariably, she considered everything. It was wonderful to see this woman, full of doubt and insecurity develop into a confident, articulate writer.

There is no doubt in my mind that her subject matter wore her down. She wanted to be, as she put it, 'a proper author', writing about big issues and events. She wanted to look up and away from her own preoccupations. And then again, she relished reading her stories aloud at writers' circles. The sound of her voice and her face, the layers of irony and menace are hard to forget. At times she saw her gift as a curse, and at other times she saw this curse as a gift.

Frances died in 1991, aged forty-four years. She was more settled than she had been since *No Mate for the Magpie* was published. She found difficulty in dealing with praise and acclaim. She felt in some way that it was undeserved. No-one could have been more critical of her than she was with herself. She hid this from most people. Her life was taking a new course when she was unexpectedly taken ill. She had a stroke and died on March 28th. Holy Thursday.

Gerard Brady

About the stories

Frances Molloy's debut novel, *No Mate for the Magpie*, is a *tour de force*, perhaps one of the most original fictional responses to the Troubles to come out of Northern Ireland. It established her as a witty and ironic storyteller, who was not afraid to use dialect, and could make exquisite use of that most subtle of storytelling devices, the *faux-naif* narrator. In the novel her intrepid heroine, Ann Elizabeth McGlone grows up working class, catholic and female in the Northern Ireland of the sixties and seventies, taking all the bigotry, cruelty and injustice she encounters in her stride.

Writing humorously came easy to Frances Molloy and she loved to make her readers laugh. But she worried that being funny might detract from the novel's more serious, satirical purpose and allow her work to be labelled as merely entertaining. This collection puts that fear to rest. There is light and dark here in a way that there was not in *No Mate for the Magpie*. These stories allow us a fuller picture of the writer, her craft and her preoccupations. They demonstrate that humour was just one of many devices which she could employ to make her point. For while they cover similar territory to *No Mate for the Magpie*, and portray a similar kind of people (the disempowered, the damaged, and the wronged), they do so by drawing on a much broader spectrum of story-telling techniques and a much broader range of emotions.

For instance, the collection opens with 'An Irish fairytale', a droll story which somehow manages to sound loquacious in less than three hundred words, outing 'holy St Kevin' as the patron saint of 'woman beaters' in the process. The book closes with a much longer, traditional narrative, 'The devil's gift' (which, like most of the stories here, is not written in dialect). This story is an elaboration of an episode from *No Mate for the Magpie*. It follows a novice nun's tortuous initiation into the Church in obsessive detail. Here an innocent sense of right and a corrupt embodiment of power meet head on. Who triumphs? This is left for the reader to decide. Molloy's own sympathies are clear. By letting the novice better her haughty superior (the ironically named Mother Virtue) in moral debate, she allows us as readers some sense of poetic justice. The two stories could not be more different in style, yet they share the same concerns. Both explore misogyny and the abuse of power within religious institutions.

In many of the stories the dark is not kept at bay. We find ourselves right in the heart of it in stories like 'The last thing' and 'Only the innocent'. In each of these a young individual (female in one story, male in the other) is isolated, sexually abused and condemned to loneliness for the rest of their lives by the value system they (or their intended partner) learnt in childhood. In such stories we feel Frances Molloy's passionate concern for the damaged and the wronged. She does not give us happy endings. We leave these stories raging against injustice and the manipulation of the young and naive. As she puts it so tellingly, 'only the innocent can believe they are evil... only the corrupt can convince them.'

These stories require us to reassess Frances Molloy's art. In some ways they have a greater reach than *No Mate for the Magpie*. Their concerns and narrative treatment locate her work alongside that of authors with whom she formerly seemed to have little in common – such as Mary Beckett, Maeve Kelly and even early John McGahern. But there are distinct differences too. Molloy's voice tends to be more obsessive. Her technique tends to be more dramatic. She explores her chosen themes (or the themes that chose her) with a tenacity akin to that of Flannery O'Connor. Both she and O'Connor focused on a relatively narrow band of experience. They shared a passion for and fidelity to their characters. Jane Austen described her terrain as a 'little bit (two inches wide) of Ivory'. Frances Molloy's two inches of ivory is the south Derry countryside, its people and their mores, during the nineteen-fifties and sixties.

This, of course, could be an intensely confined space. A sense of entrapment is a common denominator for many of her characters. And physical entrapment is nearly always accompanied by a psychological entrapment. In 'The Godmother', Frances Molloy's first ever short story, a grown daughter struggles to make her narrow-minded mother understand what a deliverance it was for her to be shown the city of Derry by a kindly local taxi driver. This opens the horizons of a girl who, 'At fourteen years a age... hadn't been out the foot a the town.' The story hinges on the mother's misplaced suspicions and the daughter's intuitive understanding of her own situation. As a child she kept her special day a secret, knowing that to tell would be to have the experience rendered sinful. The profoundest irony in this simple dialogue lies in the revelation that the priest, and not the supposed reprobate, turns out to be the person most deserving of suspicion.

Frances Molloy's determination to 'show' rather than 'tell' the plight of the oppressed is nowhere better demonstrated than in the title story, a wonderful dramatic monologue which teems with irony, using differing levels of awareness between reader and character to create a monster – an unrepentant abuser who condemns himself without being aware of it as he speaks. This approach invites the reader to empathise with his voiceless victim, amplifying the horror we feel for his wife's situation. Reading this story is one of the most chilling experiences in the book.

While many of the central characters are female, I think that gender was not of crucial significance for the author. Violence against and violation of the rights of the individual are her uppermost concern. In these pages young men and women, boys and girls suffer in isolation – sometimes through their own ignorance but more often at the hands of the powerful, be they parents, teachers, priests, employers, conmen or nuns. Supposed places of safety, such as the family, are often the places of greatest risk and censure. Frances Molloy's portrayal of Irish country folk is not unlike John Steinbeck's depiction of the rural poor in California at the time of the great depression. Both are friends of the poor and of those who naively stand up to what they sense is wrong, or, sadly, go under as a consequence of that wrong.

But this is not the whole picture. Escape is possible. Some measure of autonomy is achieved in the last two stories, 'The fortune teller' and 'The devil's gift'. And some of the stories, such as 'Dancing with my daddy', a touching and funny correspondence between a young internee and a schoolgirl, are full of gentle humour and affection. One of the most satisfying of these stories is 'A bee in a bottle'. It is a sheer joy to read, a fond recollection of childhood and a moving, poetic tribute to her father.

These stories were not written as a collection, nor do they appear here in chronological order. Some were written before, some during, and about half after *No Mate for the Magpie*. She did not begin with conventional forms and move to the experimental. She wrote both side by side: narrative realism, monologue, fable, reminiscence, dialect and correspondence all have a place in this collection.

As a collection these stories are easy to read but hard to digest. They remind us of the kind of realities that lie behind the daily headlines, the same yesterday, today and, unfortunately, tomorrow. For Frances Molloy's art is wholly concerned with highlighting human damage and human resilience, not in any prescriptive way, but in a way that allows the characters and their dilemmas to speak for themselves, with a colloquial eloquence. Although she spent most of her adult life away from Ireland, nearly everything she wrote was set there, with only one of her last stories, 'The fortune teller', taking on a different location and feel. This might have seemed to mark out a new direction, but she subsequently returned to Irish based work. It would seem that, like ill-starred Ann McGlone, Frances Molloy's muse 'would never quite escape the compellin' god-forsaken shores 'of my fool-driven land'.'

Ruth Carr

An Irish fairytale

Once upon a time, in the land of saints and scholars, there lived a handsome young man named Kevin. One day he decided to retreat from the world and spend the rest of his life giving praise to God as a holy hermit. He then went to live high up on a ledge in a wild remote place indeed, called Glendalough, in the county of Wicklow. Now, there was also, at the same time, in the land of saints and scholars, a beautiful maiden, whose name is forgotten on account of the fact that it was never considered worth remembering. Well, didn't this beautiful maiden fall madly in love with the holy hermit. She made lots of attempts to talk to him, to get him to come down off his lonely ledge, for she wanted him to fall in love with her too and come away down and marry her. He didn't want to at all so he did a lot of praying, meditating, and confabbing with God, and after he was finished he decided to put an end to her wooing. And he did. The next time she came up to him he shoved her down off the top of his high ledge and she got broke into smithereens on the rocks far down below, and God was very pleased with the holy hermit. When he died, many years later, as an old, old, man, the people of Ireland acclaimed him a saint. And ever since, droves of nuns, from all over Ireland have converged on his tomb, annually, every year, to pray for the great virtue of chastity as practised by holy Saint Kevin, the patron saint of woman beaters.

Maggie's day out

After six years of marriage Maggie decided to have a day out. To be more correct, I should say that after she had been married for six years her mother decided that it was high time Maggie had a day out. Maggie went along with the idea – almost enthusiastically. It was decided that she should go on a Sunday, as that day was the most convenient for all concerned. When the big day arrived her mother and brother called to take her to Portstewart in the same car that had taken her unconscious husband to the hospital, after he had collapsed on hearing the false report that Maggie had died in childbirth, less than a year after she married him. Tucked away in the back seat of their Bluebird she sped off with a last nervous wave to her husband and the three children, who stood watching agog, never having seen anything quite like this before. The idea that their mother could voluntarily absent herself from their company, for a whole day, had never ever occurred to them.

She wasn't long gone before her husband began to busy himself with the main task before him, making dinner for himself and the children. Maggie had been up at the crack of dawn to make the breakfast early, in order that his work should be lighter, for she knew that he had no natural propensity for anything domestic. In his own way, Jamie too looked forward to the day. He had watched Maggie carefully the week before when she had made a stew. It was only a question of chopping up some meat and vegetables, putting them in a saucepan, covering them with salty water and letting them boil for a while. Changing the nappy on the baby, who was one year old, would have been a tricky enough business he felt, if Maggie had not taught the two older children how it was done. Still, he had a part to play because Maggie had threatened to call the whole trip off if he didn't promise to remove the pin from the soiled nappy and replace it in the clean one, after the children had changed it. Changing nappies, Jamie believed, was strictly women's work. He went so far as to tell himself, that if Maggie ever died on him he would send the baby to the Nazareth nuns sooner than change a shitty nappy. Apart from this unpleasant operation Jamie could foresee no real problems as he started early to prepare the dinner.

At twelve o'clock the stew was ready, and Jamie, being a great believer in cutting corners wherever possible, bade his children be seated on the floor on top of the folded coats which he had placed there for that purpose. He poured the stew into a large baking bowl and with spoon in hand sat down on the floor feeding the children and himself a spoonful at a time, until the lot of it was gone. His two eldest children, Tommy and Mary readily agreed that food had never tasted quite so nice before. Jamie told them proudly that he planned many another day like this one. Their mother's work would be cut by half he boasted, after she took to his way of doing things. There would be no more need to wash up dirty dishes or clear the table after a meal. With a bit of forward thinking beforehand, all that drudgery would be avoided. After his triumph with the dinner Jamie kept the children in stitches for a full half hour, for he was a great weaver of comic tales. The baby crying for a nappy change put a stop to all his gaiety. He removed the pin with much distaste and let the children get on with the rest of the operation. When this unpleasant task was completed Jamie sent Tommy and Mary out to play, as far from the house as possible in order that the baby might sleep undisturbed. As soon as they were gone he placed himself in his favourite chair and carried on with his usual Sunday afternoon amusement, reading cowboy books which he rented by the dozen from a barber in the village.

Tommy and Mary had never had so much freedom before. Their mother, instead of sending them far away from the house, insisted that they stay very quiet when the baby was asleep. She always rewarded them for their silence afterwards with a saucer full of raisins but they both preferred their father's way. He had said there were going to be lots of other days like this one. The world was beginning to open out for them. They climbed over gates and fences and squeezed through hedges formerly forbidden. They peeped into the well where their mother warned them never to go for fear the bogey-man who lived in the water should come and take them down below.

As far as the eye could see in every direction from where they stood, the fields were full of stooks of corn, standing like minute thatched tepees, golden, as if in some unwritten fairy tale. Tommy tried to jump over one but it was much too high, so it was quite by accident that he discovered what fun could be had by jumping on a stook and bringing it down. Two hours later, not a single stook still stood. Tired at last of this game the children went exploring, searching for treasure. The only thing their quest turned up was a bottle of crude oil, left behind in a hedge by some farmer. They were about to discard it as uninteresting when Tommy remembered something he heard from a big boy at school about oil not mixing with water. This had long puzzled Tommy so he brought their find to the well, to see what would happen. If they both suspected at the offset of this adventure that oil could mix very well with water, they forgot about it very soon in their delight on seeing the many patterns and colours that appeared before their eyes on the surface of the well. Tommy knew the names of lots of colours and he listed them to Mary and pointed them out with the end of his stick.

They were so wrapped up in their discovery that they did not see their father until he was upon them, standing looking down with his face puffed in rage. He gave Tommy a hard kick that nearly sent him flying into the well. He grabbed

Tommy by the hair and lifted him clean off the ground, before hitting him hard on the face. He threw him on the ground again and kicked him some more. Mary ran away then and hid in a hedge and prayed for Tommy. After a long time when it was getting dark she heard her father's voice calling her name but she was silent in fear for her life. When at last he found her, he was like himself again – gentle. He lifted her up onto his shoulders and carried her home. He put her in bed beside her brother. Tommy did not look like himself anymore. He could not talk. Their father made them cocoa and told them to drink it all. He was kinder than ever then. Tommy tried hard to do what he was told but he vomited every time he took a sip. Jamie lifted Tommy out of bed and carried him about the floor. He told him that he never meant to hurt him and only wanted everything to be right for his mammy coming home. He said he didn't know what came over him when he lost his temper but that he would make it up to Tommy every day for the rest of his life. He said nobody would ever know how sorry he was.

When Maggie came home that night and found out what had happened to Tommy she didn't go away again for another fourteen years, and when she did she took Jamie with her.

Only the innocent

He looked away from the woman's legs and fixed his gaze on the train in the next siding. The light, missing the cavity of a dent on the engine carriage, looked like Charlie Chaplin's head, hat at a jaunty angle. The woman whose legs his eyes had followed came in and sat down in the seat opposite. He blushed faintly, waited for a respectable time to elapse, then rose and moved to another seat further along on the opposite side of the aisle.

Rail tracks stretched away to his right like freshly ploughed rows of dark earth, glinting in the weak, early morning sunlight. He could almost smell the soil. Forty years dropped from his memory. He was a small boy again, walking behind a farmer all the way up a field, always keeping two steps behind, watching the horse, listening to its panting, marvelling at the cleft the old plough made in the earth and the way it effortlessly curled it over. The top of the world going underneath and the underearth appearing on top, a flock of flapping birds forever at their heels, scavenging for worms.

The farmer would sometimes ask, 'What is your da doing these days, son? Over about the old granda's, is he?' But mostly they'd never speak a word. They'd just tread silently up and down, up and down, listening to the earth groaning as the glinting rows of black soil lined up, one at the back of the other, and the horse panted and sweated and wore himself out with the constant toil, like a mother.

Thinking back made him feel fidgety but he could not stop

himself. He looked down at his hands and put them away in his pockets. 'The devil always finds work for idle hands,' his mother used to tell him. Twenty-five years dead now, his mother. The soil they put over her was sticky and brown; choking soil, not a glint of the sun to be seen on it anywhere. 'Remember man that thou art dust,' the priest had said over her coffin. 'She is not a man,' he wanted to shout. 'Not a man. She is my mother. She is the one I betrayed.' I let him talk to me about her. I talked to him about her.

Then the face. The face. The face of the man. The face of the man he had betrayed her with, formed before his eyes again and settled itself on the face of the priest in that moment of final insult. The man. The man, black-clad and sinister, stood at the side of her grave and told her last remains to 'remember' that she was a 'man'. That was the day his faith died. His faith in God. He had no faith left in men. Women. Women were different. Women were clean. But he was sullied. Dirtied. Excluded from relations with women forever.

'Tickets please,' the guard called, moving along the aisle. He fumbled and found his in the breast pocket of his jacket. The train moved on through the flat English Midlands. He turned his tired eyes towards the window again. Smoke rose from early morning chimneys. Ramshackle factories, where he once would have found work, were closed up and crumbling. He saw plastic bin-liners caught in hedges, heaped carcasses of old cars and scrap metal. The approach of another town. Streetlights burning dimly in the sunshine. Concrete slags, intended for some forgotten building scheme, broken up, discarded. Locked-up churches. Overgrown graveyards.

Nobody to attend her grave now. He tried to blot the past out. Tried. Failed. His father coming home drunk beating her up. Calling her unspeakable names. She lived in terror of him. They all did. Himself. His brothers. His sisters. He didn't know where any of them were now. His brothers and sisters. Didn't know whether they were alive or dead. Even his sister, the nun. If she was alive she would be praying for him, poor soul.

Apart from Father Curry, she was the only one he had told. She was older than him and always so kind and wise. He went to her for advice. Comfort. Answers. She had none. Just sat there, looking at him oddly. Trying to say things that didn't come. Mumbling about how awful it must have been. He had been a fool to tell her. A woman couldn't understand. It had frightened her into a convent.

He was thirteen that day and had had the stirrings of sin in himself for nearly a year then. But he prayed hard and worked hard and fought off the impure thoughts that had started to plague him for no reason that he could understand. Then he met the man. The man. The man. When he was thirteen. The man came to the town two days a week. He had a store up a back alley. He sold second-hand furniture. He had never met the man before that day but his mother had often bought bits and pieces of furniture off him. The man met him in the street and recognised him.

'Are you Mrs —'s son?' the man asked.

'Yes,' he said.

'She's a lovely woman. You take after her,' the man said.

He was delighted. He smiled at the man.

'Thanks,' he said. He hated to think that he might take after his father.

'She's a good customer of mine too,' the man said.

He glowed with pride. His father never said anything nice about his mother though he himself thought her the loveliest woman on earth.

'She was asking after a chest of drawers the last time she was in,' the man said. 'I have one at the moment, cheap. Would you like to look at it for her?'

He followed the man up the alley and into the store in the yard. The man locked the door behind them, once they were inside.

'It's away up at the back,' the man said. 'I can't go in there without locking the place. I have a lot of valuable stuff in here.' The man led the way. He followed after. The man showed him a chest of drawers.

'Cheap. Very cheap, tell her,' the man said.

He thanked the man politely for taking the trouble and turned to go.

'Don't be rushing off,' the man said. 'I'm making a cup of tea. I've got some nice biscuits. You might as well have a sup with me when you're here. Sit there. I won't be a minute.'

He sat where he was told, on a red sofa. The man made tea and talked to him about his mother. He talked to the man about his mother. Yes, she was a brave woman. Yes, she deserved better. Yes, he would look after her when he was grown up.

'You'll not have long to wait now,' the man said, 'you're nearly grown up as it is. I suppose you're already out chasing the girls?'

He blushed. The man sat down beside him, left the tea on the floor and put his hand on his knee.

'No need to be embarrassed,' the man said. 'Nothing wrong with liking girls.'

He blushed more. It was happening again. He could feel it. Stirring. Starting to grow. Like it did when he was in bed at night and visions of girls crowded his mind. He couldn't pray then. The man was talking to him. Asking would he like to see photos of girls. He tried to stop himself saying 'yes' but could not. The man took photos from his pocket. He took the photos from the man. He couldn't believe what he saw. Naked girls lying and sitting on beds and on sofas. Men doing things to them. He was ashamed of what he was looking at, but the sin that was stirring in him took possession of him. The man took the pictures from him and left them on the chest of drawers. The man's eyes had a strange look. He grabbed him, pushed him into a corner and forced his face into a mouldy rolled-up carpet. The man held him gagged there, unbuttoned his trousers, pulled them down and did it to him.

'You're a dirty little bastard, aren't you?' the man said.

'You liked that, didn't you?'

'No.'

'Of course you did.'

Silence. The boy started to cry.

'If you say a word about this to anyone I'll tell them it was you. You started it. You got me going. You're a dirty little bastard and you know it.'

He limped away. He didn't know what to do. He went to the chapel and begged God's forgiveness, accused himself of vile things.

Next day he confessed to Father Curry. His protector.

'Forgive me, father.'

'Forgive you,' the priest said. 'You have committed one of the sins that cry to heaven for vengeance. First, wilful murder. Second, sodomy. Third, oppression of the poor. Fourth, depriving the labourer of his wages.'

'Which one have I committed, father?'

'Sodomy,' Father Curry spat. 'You have sullied your soul forever.'

He never went back to confession again. There was no point. The priest was a saint. A walking saint, his mother always told him. So he left that confession, carrying with him a sin that could never be forgiven. That is what frightened him into telling his sister. That is what turned her into a Poor Clare, locked away behind high walls, praying for him night and day.

He left for England three years later when he was sixteen but he couldn't settle anywhere for long. All the time working, a few months in one town and then moving on to another. Never allowing himself to be idle. Always shunning, shamefully, the society of women. Believing himself to be tainted.

But trains always stopped and always stopped in seedy places. When the train came to a halt at the next take-away town where he hoped to find work, he got off and his past limped along behind him. He would carry the hurt of what happened that day all through his life, like a lame dog carries an injured paw, never able to figure out that he was not to blame. That only the innocent can believe they are evil. That only the corrupt can convince them.

The happy wife

No one could have been more miserable than she. At night she lay awake for hours thinking about him. His doings with others. He hardly ever touched her now unless he was too drunk to care. And the humiliation of having to go out with him and suffer his insults in public was never worth what happened afterwards. She planned to change everything. Do something. One of these days she would find a way to change him. He would stop doing it with them and do it with her again.

It was not women he was doing it with now, no not women. She had stood up for herself against them long ago. He wouldn't dare talk to a woman now. He had been very free and easy with women in the past but she had put a stop to that. She had been less successful in preventing him from getting pally with men. She had not made allowance for that particular bent. He was screwing other men and being screwed by them – the filth, the vulgarity, the ugliness of it. He was having all that fun and she was having none. He was her man, her man, her man. She hated him for doing it, doing it, all the time doing it and not doing it with her.

She planned to change him, change him, but how? The doctor, she would go to the doctor. Tell him everything. He would give her something to make her man normal. Something to make him want to do it with her instead of them.

She went to the doctor. She sat in the crowded waiting-room getting it all straight in her mind, thinking of what she would say to the doctor, a nice man the doctor. A normal man the doctor. The doctor didn't do it with them, he did it with his wife. The doctor was happy. The doctor's wife was happy. She alone was miserable, miserable because of him, because he didn't do it with her. Because he was having a good time doing it with them.

When her turn came she entered the consulting room. She took the seat the doctor offered. A nice man, a gentle man, a caring, soothing man, a nice quiet-mannered man. She told the doctor of her plight. The doctor listened and looked concerned. She told him that her man never done it with her. She told him what she knew – that he was doing it with them. She cried to the doctor. She told him of the other cases of abnormality that had occurred in his family. The doctor sat with bowed head. The doctor had heard it all before. He told her what he told the others. That tablets would not fix him. He told her that her man was not a homosexual. He told her not to worry because some men done it less often than others. He told her that the reason why her man wasn't keen on doing it with her was because her man was under-sexed. He had very little libido.

She brightened up and smiled. She felt very grateful to the doctor. Less miserable for having talked. She admired the doctor for his gentleness, his caring, soothing manner and was positively astounded by his wisdom. She thanked the doctor and left his room happy. It was amazing how wrong you could be. Amazing what you could make yourself believe. Now that she understood she could start enjoying herself. Make friends with people he liked, be friendly with people she had been rude to. In the past when his friends had invited them to their homes she had made them fully aware she disliked them. She had been wrong, dreadfully wrong. She would not do that again, no not now, now that she knew the truth, that he could not be doing it with them – that she had been mistaken in that particular view. Now that she knew why he didn't do it with her she felt a momentary tinge of shame. But above all, she was happy, blissfully happy, because she knew that he could not be doing it – with anybody.

Women are the scourge of the earth

There's some people who will try to put the blame for what happened on to me but I'm not having that. I don't care what that note said. I don't care what the neighbours say. If they think I give a damn, then they're mistaken. That woman was unbalanced all her life. She'd been taking tablets for years from doctors for her nerves. Feared to let the wains out to play in case they got shot. Silly woman – I told her to catch herself on. If anybody wanted to shoot the bloody wains they could come into the house and do it.

I don't care what any of them try to tell you – I never lifted a finger to her in all the years I put up with her. Never mine what that hussy next door tries to make out. The stories I could tell you about her. You should see the odd assortment of characters that come and go there when he's out at his work, the poor bugger. There's no telling who or what fathered that crowd of cross-eyed brats of hers. I must say, it's always people like her who do the talking. I can't imagine what kind of a man he is at all to put up with it. She should be run out of the town. Many a better woman was tarred and feathered for far less. Shooting is too good for the likes of her.

That note that the missus left made out that I turned her mother and her sisters against her, but unbalanced and all as she was, she was fly enough not to mention why. Well, I'll tell you why, so you'll not be labouring under any illusions about her. She was carrying on with a fancy man. A friend of mine spotted the same car parked outside my house on the same day every week and gave me the wink. I soon put a stop to it I can tell you. I knocked his teeth right down his throat and let it be known that I would debollocks the bastard on the spot if he ever came snooking around my house again. I'll not be made a laughing stock of.

Her mother was fuming mad when I told her the way her precious daughter was carrying on. She said the missus was no daughter of hers and that she'd never darken her door again the longest day she ever lived and to give the woman her dues, she was as good as her word. All her sisters took my side in the matter too.

You would think that she would toe the line after that but by the blood of the crucified Jesus, God forgive me for taking the holy name, didn't she go more deranged than ever after that. She'd walk through the house in a stupor half the day, never even bothering to change from her night clothes. She was pining for him. You didn't need to be very clever to see that. All the time she kept pretending that it was her mother and her sisters that she wanted to see and she kept on asking me to go back to them and explain that she didn't have a fancy man, that he was only her friend. I told her that it was herself who had got into the mess and it was up to her to get herself out of it. I'm not going to be made a fool of.

I'm here to defend my good name, never mine your inquest. The woman was deranged, that's the long, the tall, and the short of it. I lived with her for fifteen years and I'm telling you now, she was never in her proper mine. I don't know what I was ever thinking about, having anything to do with the likes of her in the first place when I think of some of the women I could have had me pick of. I could have done a lot better for myself and married a good, strapping farmer's daughter with a bit of capital behind her. Indeed, I'll have you all know, I could have had any woman I wanted, just for the asking.

And here's another thing I want to draw your attention to, just when you're at it. A woman is supposed to obey her husband, is she not? She's supposed to do what he bids her, is she not? Isn't that what the law says? Isn't it? And isn't it wrote in the bible by the hand of the almighty Himself? Well, that woman never did my bidding in her life. Never once in fifteen years could I get her to do my bidding. For example, I told her to keep away from your woman next door. I didn't want no wife of mine consorting with the likes of her. But did she heed me? Like hell, she did. My friend seen that trollop from next door in having tea with her ladyship when ever I was out at my work. My blood still boils when I think of it – the likes of that trash sitting gossiping in my house and me out breaking my back to earn the money to entertain her. I soon put a stop to that, mine. I locked the outside doors to the house and took the keys with me to work for a week or so and made it known to the madam next door that if she wanted to visit my house she could try getting in and out the windows. I'll have you know, I won't be made a fool of.

And another thing she done you ought to know – she turned them five wains of hers against me. Not one of them has a decent word to say about their father now. That wee uppity lying bitch Una went away and told the doctors yarns behine my back. What do you think of that for respect then? Going away behine my back and in defiance of my orders, bringing doctors round the house to see the mother. That woman would be alive today if she'd seen far fewer doctors. It was all the fool tablets that she got from them that made her fall, that's where she got her bruises from, I never laid a finger on her in me life.

Una has turned into a right uppity wee brat and she would need to mine her step. She'll not always have the old grannie's skirts to hide behine. Just let her wait till all this fuss dies down. A man has a legal right to his own wains. I'll have her know before I'm through, who's the boss in our house. Who does she think puts the clothes on her back? Who does she think puts the food in her belly? Who does she think's been paying the rent all these bloody years? The beloved fancy man, Uncle Harry?

What do you think of that then, Uncle Harry? Uncle Harry,

if you don't mine. She brought her dear Uncle Harry round to her old granny to poison her mine against me. Me and the mother-in-law had always got on well enough – I'm not saying that she wasn't a terrible old battle-axe, for she was, but as the man says, I didn't have to live with her. That woman has known me these eighteen years or more and still, she's prepared to take the word of a complete stranger before mine. What do you think of that for loyalty then? I suppose she thinks she's mixing in high-brow society now because he works in an office and dresses in pansy clothes.

But you haven't heard the best of it, no, not by a long shot. Wait till you hear the story the brave fellow is trying to put about. He's trying to make out that he met me missus at a meeting of some daft organization, what's this it's called now, let me think? It's for a lot of these people who has been let out of the funny-farm. 'Mental' or something, it's called. No, that's not right I think, nor was it called 'insane' either because it started with an 'm' I'm sure of that now. 'Mine', that's what it's called, it's for people that's out of their mines. 'Mine', 'Mine', that's what its name is, didn't I say it began with an 'm'. You see, I was right.

The bold uncle Harry told me mother-in-law that me missus was suffering from depression and that's why she joined this daft shower of freaks. He tries to make out that he was suffering from depression too and that's how the two of them met. According to his story, they were only friends and it helped them to meet for a chat and a cup of tea once a week. What do you think of that for invention? Isn't that very touching wouldn't you say? They were only good friends indeed. I'd say he must have been very hard up for a friend if he had to rely on her.

The old granny must be starting to dote, for didn't she swallow the whole story, lock, stock and barrel. You should hear her lamenting now about how she should never have doubted for a second the virtue of her lily-white daughter. All he called for was a chat and a cup of tea. What does he take me for, a real dodo? That's the kind of a story nobody but an old doting woman would fall for.

A quare lot she had to be depressed about I can tell you, with a mug like me out humping bricks on his back all day long to keep her in style. Carpets in every room, that woman had. When I think about it yet, my blood still boils. Me out slaving to provide grandeur for her to impress her fancy man with.

I'll tell you this now, she's the last woman I'll ever work for. Women, they're all the same – after what they can get out of you. There's only one thing a woman is useful for and that's on the broad of her back and nobody but a fool would marry a woman for that. There's plenty of that going free and no mistaking. Women are the scourge of the earth. I'm well rid of her. I've learnt my lesson. Once bitten, twice shy, as the man says.

Dancing with my daddy

June 25th 1957

Dear Danny,

My name is Kate and my daddy is in jail with you. He asked me to write to you because you would like a pen-pal. He said me and my brother was to write to you. I am ten and a half and my brother is eleven and three quarters. My brother is called John and he says that I have to write first and see what happens. He's a right coward, our John. How long have you been in the jail? My daddy has been in for two months. You are my first pen-pal. One time I wrote a letter to Pudsy Ryan in Our Boys but he didn't answer me.

    Yours faithfully

    Kate Kelly. (Miss)

July 2nd 1957

Dear Kate,

Thanks a million for writing to me. Your daddy said he would ask you to write but I never imagined it would happen. You have no idea how much it meant to me to receive your letter. I carry it around with me everywhere and read it three or four times a day. Your daddy laughs at me for reading it so often. He says that I'm only a big wain. The days in here are very long as you can imagine, with nothing to do and nowhere to go. I've been in six months but it seems more like sixty years. I share a cell with your daddy and another internee called Jim, who comes from Belfast. He plays a flute and he has your daddy and me round the bend with his practising. Your daddy says he ought to go away and join up with an Orange band, but he can be good crack sometimes too, telling jokes, though I find it hard to understand the Belfast accent. I'm the youngest internee in the Crumlin. You don't need me to tell you how awful that can be. Everybody teases me about it. Sometimes I cry, it gets so bad. Then your daddy tells them to leave me alone. I don't know what I would do without him. He's my best friend in here.

I hope you will write back to me. I will write to you again but I can't write as often as I'd like because I'm only allowed to send two letters a week. I write one to my mother and one to my sister, Sheila. You would like her. She's married and has two little boys. I miss them all a lot. My father, R.I.P., died last December. It would be nice if you could get your brother John to write as well. Your daddy talks all the time about you two. One day I hope to meet you both with your mammy and all the little ones when I get out of this place.

I'll soon have to finish as I'm coming to the end of my paper. We are only allowed two sheets of paper per week but can get in as many letters as people like to send us. I'll be waiting to hear from you. Tell me all the things that are happening out there and tell me what you do all day. Give my best wishes to your mammy and John and all the family. Your daddy is in the pink, T.G.

Your pen-pal,
Danny.

July 5th 1957

Dear Danny,
It was great to get your letter. I knew it was from you, even before I opened it because it had the Crumlin stamped on it and I could tell it wasn't my daddy's writing. Daddy tells us you were very good at school and would have gone far if they hadn't lifted you. How is daddy keeping? Mammy was up

seeing him last week. She says he is getting very old looking. You're very lucky you can see him every day. I wish I was you. I went to school today and the teacher gave me a good hiding because I hadn't been to school for three weeks. She pretended she forgot my name. I told her and she made me say it again out loud so as everybody could hear. She held her hand round the back of her ear and pulled it forward. She always does that when I speak. All the other wains were laughing. 'And why have you decided to grace us with your presents, Miss Kelly?' she said. I didn't know what she was talking about so my face went all red and I said, 'Sorry Miss, I didn't know I was supposed to bring presents.' I got ten of the best. You only get ten of the best for not knowing your catechism or stuttering or doing something awful. A boy got ten of the best last year for calling Derry, Londonderry. The next day his mother came to the school and gave the teacher a good wigging. All the wains were clapping and cheering and egging her on. She was bigger than the teacher and the boys were shouting, 'Take the cane to her, Missus Doherty. Beat her black and blue. Kill her.' The teacher got her hair all pulled out of her bun but she didn't get a licking with the cane. At the time, I felt sorry for her. The boy never came back near the school again. They say that he died with the trouncing that the teacher gave him. I wish mammy would go to the school and give her a good wigging for me. It would serve her right. That is all for now. John says he is going to write to you soon. I would write you a longer letter only that my hands is still sore.

Yours faithfully,
Kate Kelly.

July 9th 1957

Dear Kate,

I'm writing straight back to you instead of to my sister, Sheila. She is so busy with the two little ones that she barely has time to read my letters anyway so I'm sure she'll forgive this once.

That school you go to sounds worse than the jail. I would like to get my hands on that teacher of yours. I enjoyed the description of the boy's mother giving her a good wigging, but couldn't make out all your writing. What did you say about 'kicking' her 'bum'? Whatever happened to her, she deserved. Why should you feel sorry for an old tinker like that? There's not much strange going on here. Everybody is the same. We got two new internees in last week but they're both from the Free State. They don't have much truck with us Northerners. You would sometimes think we were hooks by the way they go on. I suppose everyone likes to stick with their own kind.

The only excitement that has happened round here since I last wrote, is that some of the lads have seen Alfie Hinds. It shows how exciting this place is. The whole talk here has been about him. You know, they say he's innocent, and the lads believe he should be let out. After all the lights are turned off at night in the cells, they chant away for hours, 'Release the internees, release the political prisoners, release Alfie Hinds.' It sets up some racket, I can tell you. It keeps me awake. I hear that Hinds has to wear a prison uniform, not like us. They say he is a very dapper looking man all the same. If you're innocent, I suppose you must look innocent, no matter what they do to you. It must be even lonelier for him in here than it is for us, with nobody at all to talk to. The screws take him out twice a day, to walk round the exercise yard, the only Englishman in the Crumlin.

I've run out of paper again. Your daddy is in the pink, thank God. Keep away from that old teacher of yours.

Your pen-friend,
Danny.

August 4th 1957

Dear Danny,
I was delighted to get your letter and hear that my daddy is in the pink. I'm sorry you couldn't make out all my writing. I laughed when I read your letter. I didn't say anything about

'kicking' or 'bum'. What I wrote was, licking and bun. Round here a good licking means a good beating, and what you must have mistook for bum was bun, you know, the thing that women put their hair up in? The reason you cannot make out my writing is that I'm left handed, but I write with my right hand. I used to do everything with my left hand but bless myself, before I started school. But when I went to school, the teacher stood up facing the communion class and blessed herself with her left hand so I started doing it the way the teacher was doing it. The other wains watching her did it the way my mammy did it and the teacher beat me. When I told mammy, she beat me too because I blessed myself with the wrong hand and the teacher and mammy both said that the left hand was the hand of the devil so I do everything with my right hand and that's why you can't read my writing. The teacher still blesses herself with the left hand. Well, you'll be glad to hear that I don't have to go to the old school again for a long time because the summer holidays is on. I hope you don't mind me asking about something I didn't understand in your letter. What is 'hooks' and 'screws'? Our John says they have something to do with carpentry but I don't believe him. He says to tell you that he will write to you real soon. I hope my daddy is doing well. Tell him I was asking for him. I'll have to close now because mammy says I've been writing long enough. I hope you are in the pink. I'll write to you again soon.

Your faithful pen-pal,
Kate.

August 16th 1957

Dear Kate,
As always it was great to get your letter. I was glad to hear that you wouldn't have to go back to the school for some time. I think you should never go back. Your letter made me laugh. Then I read your other letter and could see that you had written nothing about kicking the teacher's bum. It must have been

wishful thinking on my part that led me to read it the way I did. There's nothing wrong with your handwriting. It is very neat and nice. The reason I made a mistake with the reading is because I need specks. Your daddy and I laughed too at John's explanation of 'hooks' and 'screws'. You were right not to believe him, they have nothing to do with carpentry. 'Hooks' is the name we have for the non-political prisoners, and the warders are the 'screws'. So you can pass that information on to John. I'm still waiting eagerly for his letter.

The time drags in here. The only thing that fills the gaps between letters and visits is the talk about what we are going to do when we get out. Jim, our cell mate, is going to get married to his girlfriend, who is a nurse in the hospital next door. Your daddy says she'll not be as keen on him after he gets out having had him living next door to her all these months practising on the Orange flute. He says a man should keep all his vices well under wraps till after the wedding. Your daddy says he is going to go home and sit at the fire telling stories with your ma and all you kids gathered round him. Jim tells him he must be joking, your mammy will want to have nothing more to do with him after finding out how peaceful life has been without him all these months. I tell them that I'm going to take my girlfriend to the pictures at the A.B.C. and they ask me how much money do I think I'll have to pay to bribe her to come with me. We're only kidding each other of course, it's only for the crack.

I'll have to wind up now as you can see I'm coming to the end of my paper again. My mother says my writing is getting smaller and smaller and she will soon have to get a magnifying glass to read it. Give my love to your mammy and all the family. Tell them that your daddy is keeping well, thank God.

Your fond pen-pal,
Danny.

August 23rd 1957

Dear Danny,

Thank you for your letter. It's good to know that daddy is well, thank God. Mammy always cries when she comes back from seeing him and says he is getting very old looking. Do you think he is getting old looking? There isn't much news here at the moment. Last week we got a big parcel through the post with the Crumlin Jail, Belfast, stamped all over it. We didn't know what it was till we opened it. It was all the sweets that the internees saved up for us. We'd never seen as many sweets outside a shop in our lifes. Mammy said if we ate too many we would make ourselves sick and she was right.

I'm sorry to hear that you need specks. As you can see, I have made my writing very big so as you will not have to strain your eyes. Thanks for explaining the 'hooks' and 'screws', we had a good laugh about that. John still says that he's going to write to you but I don't believe him. The school starts again next week and mammy says she'll be glad to see the tail end of us for we have her heart broke. We must have because she bought a cane last week and brought it home and beat us all for doing nothing. She didn't really beat us for doing nothing, she beat us for laughing at her all the times in the past when we had her heart broke and she said, 'if only I had a cane'. When she arrived home with the cane, we were all shocked and didn't make a mute and then she said, 'so yous didn't believe me, well, now yous will repent' and then she beat us. We were all crying and she said 'if yous don't shut up I'll give yous all something proper to cry about' so we stopped. That's all my news for the moment. What is your girlfriend called? Do you keep a photograph of her under your pillow? Mammy said I have to go out to get a bucket of water now so I'll have to finish off. I hope your eyes doesn't get any worse. We are saying a novena for them.

Your faithful fond pen-pal,
Kate.

Dear Kate,

It was great to get your letter as always though it didn't make me laugh in the least. First, an apology. When I said I needed specks I really didn't mean that there was anything the matter with my eyes. It was only a throw away line. I have perfect eyesight, thank God. What I was trying to say was that I wasn't reading properly. Thanks anyhow for making your writing big, it was very considerate of you. Also, I have to confess that I do not have a girlfriend, so I can't tell you what her name is. It's just the way people talk in here. Everybody else has a wife or a girlfriend to talk about so I just made one up to impress the other men with. If I'm not careful, I'll end up believing it myself.

I'm sorry to hear that your mammy bought a cane. I cried when I read that bit of your letter. Your daddy asked me what was wrong and has promised me that he will write to your mammy and ask her not to use it again. I hope everything goes better for you when you go back to the school. Don't take any more nonsense from that old targe of a teacher.

At the moment all the talk here is about Christmas. Jim came up with this idea for a Christmas dance in the jail and the lads are forever on about nothing else. Do you remember I told you his girlfriend is a nurse? Well, he has fixed it up with her to ask all the nurses to come in here on Christmas Eve night to have a dance with the internees and a lot of the nurses are very keen on the idea. People have even stopped complaining about him playing his Orange flute. He's setting up a band with a few of the other lads to provide live music for the event. There has never been such excitement in the jail. The screws are even looking forward to it. All we need to do now is clear it with the matron at the Mater and the governor here at the Crumlin. I can't tell you how much I am looking forward to it. I haven't seen a single girl since I came to this place and Jim says there's some very good lookers in the Mater.

Well, that is about all the news I have at the moment. I

suppose you're right, John will never write to me. Give him my best anyhow and also your mammy and the rest of the family and say to her that I said, 'no more cane.' Your daddy is in the pink of health and he doesn't look any older that I can see, so stop worrying about him.

Your fond pen friend,
Danny.

September 15th 1957

Dear Danny,

It was good to get your letter and hear that my daddy was in the pink. I was delighted to hear that you didn't have a girlfriend. I want to be your girlfriend when I grow up. Mammy is still using the cane. She says, it's all very well for other people to talk but they don't have to put up with us twenty-four hours a day breaking her heart. She says she's harassed off the face of the earth. She gives John more beatings than the rest of us because he won't do a blessed thing he's told.

The old school's a terrible place. I get more beatings at school than I do off mammy. Last week I had to go for one day because all the class was notified about injections. The teacher said, 'I see Miss Kelly has graced us with her presents again. Would you mind telling us what you are doing here?' I said, 'Please miss, I've come for the school doctor, miss.' She said, 'What school doctor? There's no school doctor here.' I said, 'Please miss, he's going to the school at the top of the town to give everybody injections. My mammy got a letter that I had to be there.' 'What are you talking about girl?' she said. 'What school are you talking about?' I said 'The one at the top of the town where the wains wears a uniform, miss.' Then she called our John up and said, 'John Kelly, can you tell us what your sister is talking about?' He said, 'Yes miss, she means the protestant school,' and he gave me the dirtiest look. I was going to get mammy to kill him for we are not allowed to call people protestants. Mammy says it's not their fault that they haven't heard the word of God, but I didn't for fear he would get his own back on me. Our John sickens me betimes. When we were going to get the injections the other wains was teasing me and the boys threw stones at me. They said that they were giving me dancing lessons. The injection wasn't sore and the doctor called us all 'sausages' and the nurse gave us smarties off a saucer. My arm swelled up after and I got sick in the middle of the night and mammy said that these old jabs does more harm than good if the truth was known.

Mammy is not too pleased to hear about these nurses coming in to have dances in the Crumlin. She says you get all kinds of people in nursing nowadays and she has been in hospital. She said it would serve yous better if yous had some of the things to worry about that she has on her plate and that would give yous less time for dancing. I hope you don't go and take up with one of them old nurses as your girlfriend.

That is all the news for now. Our Tishy Ba took her first step on Sunday. We all clapped her and it gave her such a shock that she fell and bumped her head.

Your fond pen-friend,

Kate.

P.S. I hope my daddy is keeping in the pink.

October 5th 1957

Dear Danny,

I was sorry to get the letter from my daddy telling me that your sister Sheila is in hospital. It's alright that you can't write to me and daddy said for me to carry on writing to you all the same and you will write to me as soon as your sister is in the pink again. I lit a candle for her on Sunday and we've started a novena. Mammy says these women's problems is a terrible plague and she has suffered from them all her life. She says my turn will come too. She won't tell me what women's problems is but says I'll know soon enough. Do you know what women's problems is? Our John makes out that he knows but he won't tell me. Our John makes out that he knows everything. After our Tishy Ba took her first step and fell mammy said she wouldn't walk again for a long time because we scared her with all the carfuffle we made, but she was wrong. Tishy Ba is running around all over the house now, and mammy can hardly keep up with her.

I haven't been near the school since I last wrote so I have no news about that for you. How is things in the Crumlin? Is the nurses still coming in to have the Christmas dance? Daddy doesn't mention anything about that in his letters. It's like yous were living in two different jails.

I'll sign off now because I can't think of any more news at the moment. I will write again soon. I hope your sister is in the pink by now.

Your fond pen-friend,
Kate.

October 25th 1957

Dear Danny,

I'm sorry I didn't write to you sooner. My daddy reminded me to write again. I didn't forget about you and I carried on with the novenas and lighting candles for Sheila. Not much is happening here since I stopped getting your letters.

I only went to school one day and there was this big fight. A girl called Rosemary Carey, she's a right wee puke, fell out with this other girl called Sarah Cullen. Sarah Cullen is very quiet. I've never been talking to her but she has these nice eyes and she sometimes smiles at me. Well, Rosemary Carey said to her, 'You've got a dirty face and dirty clothes and you smell like the dunghill outside your front door. My mammy says you never had a proper bath in your life. You get dipped in a bucket. We have a proper bathroom with taps and everything. Your old Mammy has to go to the well with that old stinking bucket of yours.'

A big crowd of people was gathered. Nobody likes Rosemary Carey, she's a terrible skunner. She said to Sarah, 'My mammy says yous are all brought up bad.' Sarah said back, 'Your mammy has a lot to say for herself.' Rosemary Carey said, 'Your mammy is too busy breeding to have time to say anything.' Everybody was pushing to get to the front. 'What does that mean?' Sarah asked. 'It means your mammy is always having wains,' Rosemary Carey said.

I'll have to finish now and tell you the rest of this story in my next letter because mammy is calling me to come and help her to put the wains to bed.

Your fond pen-friend,

Kate.

November 6th 1957

Dear Kate,

Thank you for continuing to write to me while my sister was ill. I know you understand that I wanted to answer you but couldn't. All the prayers that were said for Sheila have worked wonders. At one point it was touch and go but now she is back home and well. The baby she had died, which was very sad but these things are God's will.

You were asking me what women's problems are and I can't right tell you. Your mammy would be the one to ask but I'm beginning to believe myself that men are women's problems. My sister would be the first to tell you that, if you were talking to her.

I have a lot of things to answer from your previous letters so I hope I don't leave anything out. I'm sad to know that your mammy is still using the cane. Life can't be easy for her on her own but beating you children won't make things any better for her. I'm beginning to think you would be safer in the Crumlin after all. We don't get any beatings or jabs from doctors or have people throwing stones at us. We lead a charmed life compared to you and your mammy and Sheila. All we have to worry about is the coming Christmas dance. Although the internees and the nurses are very set on the idea, we still haven't heard back from the matron or the governor. It's really up to them if the thing goes ahead, so keep your fingers crossed. And don't worry, I won't be getting a nurse as my girlfriend. I'll be lucky if I manage to ask one to dance. Tell your mammy not to worry either, it's only us young unmarried lads that are going on about this. The older men just laugh at us and say it will never come off.

Your letters are the only things that keep me sane in here. Thanks a million for writing. I look forward to hearing from you again soon.

Your loving pen-pal,
Danny.

November 6th 1957

Dear Danny,

I'll just carry on where I left off my last letter in case you are wondering what happened in the fight. Sarah Cullen said, 'Seeing as you're so good at catechism you should know that God sends my mammy wains because he loves her.' 'God doesn't send your mammy wains,' Rosemary Carey said. 'Your old daddy does that.' 'Do you think my daddy's God, then?' Sarah said and Rosemary Carey said back, 'That's a mortal sin you just said. God will strike you down dead for that. You'll get cancer. My mammy says your old daddy is only interested in the one thing. Sex.' 'What's sex then?' Sarah said. 'Sex is how your old da sends your ma all them wains,' said Rosemary. 'He makes them grow in her belly. He puts his old thing in her down where she pisses every night and she lets him.' Then Sarah flew at Rosemary Carey's throat before she could say another word and she would have strangled her there on the spot if the teacher didn't come along that minute and save her, and do you know, that old Rosemary Carey didn't even get ten of the best.

I haven't been back at the school since then and mammy says she's in no hurry to send me back again with the sort of things that be going on there. We got a letter from daddy yesterday and he says that your sister is coming home from the hospital soon so I hope you will write to me. I read all your old letters but I would like a new one now. I hope you haven't forgot me.

Your faithful pen-friend,
Kate Kelly.

Dear Danny,

Isn't it strange that we both wrote to each other on the very same day? Just think, we were maybe sitting down at the very same time of the day at the very same minute. I was all pleased to get your letter and know you hadn't forgot me. Mammy said that our letters crossed. I'm sure our letters will not cross this time because you will have to write to your sister. I'm glad she's feeling in the pink. I was sorry to hear about her baby dying. It's funny how God gives wains to some people and then takes them away again. Mammy says it's a mystery. I wonder why He does it? I suppose He must have thought that it would be too big a burden on your sister after all with her in the hospital and things. I said to mammy, I hope God doesn't take any of us away from you and you harassed off the face of the earth with us. She says I don't have to worry about the like of that. If He was going to take anybody it would be her. She hasn't had to beat any of us since she said that. She's a very bad colour our John says and we'll have to be good to her. Do you think she'll die on us? John says they'll put us into the workhouse if mammy dies and daddy away in jail.

Mammy was well pleased with the news that the dance in the Crumlin isn't for sure. She says daddy never mentioned it to her and all she ever heard of it was from your letters and it's a right herintella alltegether, nurses in the Crumlin Road jail. She said it would fit yous better yous would say your prayers to be let out instead of trying to get other people let in. She says some rare things mammy. Don't show this letter to daddy or he might tell her. How is my daddy doing? I

hope he's in the pink, please God.
　　Your faithful, fond, loving pen-friend,
　　Kate.
　　P.S. I think you and me should get married when I grow up. A boy asked me to marry him once but he was a gipsy.

December 8th 1957

Dear Danny,
I'm sorry I didn't write to you lately but we all had the flu. It was very bad. We all thought we were going to die. Mammy had to hang a sheet out on the tree at the side of the house to tell Aunt Mary that she needed her to come right away. It's because we don't have a telephone that mammy and Aunt Mary sends messages to each other on the trees. We were praying that Aunt Mary wouldn't have the flu too or we'd all be a goner. Aunt Mary never gets nothing. She fed us all on chicken broth and sent messages over to her own house on the tree to say that she was having to stay with us. They sent messages back on their tree that they were alright and she could stay as long as she was needed. That's why I didn't write to you. Why did you not write to me? I hear your sister is doing grand again. I suppose you're all busy preparing yourself for this big dance now with it being so close to Christmas. Did you get any word from the matron and the governor?
　　I'm not able to write a long letter because I'm not right better yet and I'm very tired. I hope you write back to me soon.
　　Your faithful pen-friend,
　　Kate Kelly. (Miss)

December 18th 1957

My dear Kate,
I'm sorry to say, I'm ashamed to say, that I do not have any

good excuse for not writing to you. I hope you will forgive me. I did not know that you all had the flu. I was just feeling sorry for myself and to think that after all your letters to me I couldn't even have dropped you a line and you so poorly. I'll make it up to you from now on.

Sheila is back to her usual self again, as your daddy will no doubt have told you, so I have no excuse to not answer your letters.

The only excuse I had for not writing seems so silly now. I was feeling down in the dumps because the nurses' dance is not going ahead. The governor seemed to approve alright but the matron wouldn't hear of it. You can imagine, when we got the go-ahead from the Crumlin we thought we were home and dry. The outcome isn't as bad as I thought after all, for we've decided to go ahead with the dance ourselves. It'll be good crack. The nurses have sent us a whole pile of uniforms and wigs and make up and all sorts, so half of us are dressing up as nurses and the rest of us are getting dickied up in our Sunday best and Jim and his Orange band are providing the music. Of course because I am the youngest, I have to be one of the nurses. You can imagine the teasing I'm getting about that. They tell me I'll have to shave my legs and wear nylon stockings. I didn't want to at the beginning but now I have got used to the idea it should be a great old laugh.

You kids should be getting another consignment of sweets and chocolates again soon. It's my job to collect them from the other internees and there's a lot of them. You could open your own sweet shop. Most of the men get sweets in all the time but they don't like eating them. For God's sake don't make yourself sick with them over Christmas. Too many sweets are bad for you, your mammy is right. Well Kate, I'm sadly going to have to finish off now as I'm coming to the end of my paper but I'll write to you again in the next few days as we get four extra letters for Christmas. You'll probably not get it till after the holidays now as it will doubtless be held up in the Christmas post. Take good care of yourself and have a very happy Christmas. give my best to your mammy and John and all the rest of the family.

    Your loving pen-pal,
    Danny.

December 24th 1957

Dear Danny,

I was delighted to get your lovely letter and know that you hadn't forgot me. I thought you had gone off with some old nurse and would never remember to write to me again. Mammy and us didn't tell daddy that we had the flu because we didn't want him to worry, so that is why he didn't tell you. I was delighted to hear that yous wasn't going to have no nurses in after all. Mammy says it shows that the matron is a respectable woman not like that governor of yours. She says she has never heard the like in her life, grown men dressing up in skirts. I think it's very funny. I can hardly imagine daddy dressing up as a nurse so he'll have to go as one of the men. I can just see you dancing with my daddy. I wish I was there.

    I have to keep this letter short mammy says, because we have a lot to do for tomorrow. I hope you have a very happy Christmas. I'll light a candle for you at the chapel tomorrow morning. I can hardly wait for your next letter.

    Your loving girlfriend,
    Kate *x x x.*

One more miracle

I have no right to ask, I know. I deserve it all. There's no
excuse. But I was very young. I loved him more than I
loved You. Married him outside the Church. No marriage
at all. I know that, but I was young and I am sorry now. And,
God, I am so afraid to die.

I asked him once only, would he turn with me, and his
face, God, and that little snigger. 'Turn to be a Roman Catholic?
Me a Papish? A Romanist?' I never asked him after, God. I
could not endure such ridicule twice. I shouldn't have turned
with him I know God, but he was very headstrong and wanted
his own way. Oh, I'm not making excuses for myself. I got
what I wanted too. I got the man I fell in love with, but I
turned my back on You.

And I did pray. Every day. You know that. In the early
years, continually and fervently for his conversion so that I
could become whole again. So I could be reunited with my
family, my parents, my brothers, my sisters, but it was not to
be Your holy will. First my mother died, a broken woman,
because of me. I wasn't allowed to go to her funeral. Doubly
barred by my own shameful sin. He wouldn't let me go and
my family wouldn't have me. Then my father not long after,
and now the two others, both my brothers. It will soon be my
turn and I am afraid to die.

I know I didn't deserve an answer God but I did pray. And
when they were born, my children, I baptised them catholics
secretly, intending to do as the church does. Though they

don't know it yet, they are both catholics. Always it has been my prayer that they will be spared. Do not hold against them the sins of their mother. I grew afraid of him God, that's why I didn't teach them to pray. They say all their own kind of prayers, God, the Lord's Prayer they call the Our Father, but they put the protestant piece on the end, and that worries me. It saddens me they never knew the rosary, yet I recited it every night, nor the Hail Holy Queen, the Memorare to Our Lady or the Prayer For A Happy Death.

Down the years I went with him to the protestant church on a Sunday. I even recited the protestant prayers, but not in my heart as You know. I never fully gave up my faith, I only postponed it, hoping and praying that the day would come when I could turn back towards You again, but it wasn't to be that easy. And then the years of despair when I thought You had forgotten me, and the further I strained towards Your mercy the more I experienced the gulf.

Then the greatest sin of all. Not being satisfied with my other crimes, God, I prayed to You, called out to You in my desperation to make him die. I didn't do it for myself, God, I did it for the children. You know the secrets of my heart. Only You know. Do not forsake me now, I beg You. I do not ask for mercy for myself, but if I had allowed him to know or guess what was in my heart, he would have driven me away, so great was his dislike of the church, the true church, and they would both have been lost to you forever.

When I was away from the town alone, which wasn't often, I always found a church and went to mass, but I couldn't go here for fear he would find out. Wisdom comes with age, God, and my wisdom came too late.

Oh I know in his own way he's a good man, God, and I do not want to judge. He's devoted to the children and has always provided for me. But his mistrust of catholics got stronger with every passing year, and now with these civil rights marches his hatred knows no bounds. There are times when I fear for my life. To hear the folk round here. What they wouldn't do to papishes. I can't show any sign. I pretend to be just like them but You know it's not the truth. That's all that matters to me now. You knowing.

But the real tragedy of it all is the way the children turned out. Since they have grown up, God, they're as bad almost as he. I don't know how this could have happened, or how it is going to end. I always blessed their rooms in Your name and put holy water in their tea. Praying that the grace of their baptism would eventually set their souls free.

The last thing

That was the last thing I thought. I never thought he could see it like that. It wasn't my fault. There wasn't a thing I could have done. What would you have done, tell me that? What could anybody have done? I was very young at the time, but throughout it all, that was the last thing I thought.

He went away to England to work for a year to save up for us to get married, you see, and I was well pleased with myself when this good job came along for me. It was looking after three children whose mother was dead. The man, their father, had done well for himself in business. I remember feeling sorry for him the first time I met him, thinking what a pity it was, him being left to bring up three youngsters on his own and him nearly old enough to be their grandfather.

'Since my wife died, three months ago,' he said to me at the interview, 'I've been having problems with Jean. The doctor says it's the shock of her mother's death and she'll get over it, but it's a worry all the same. You see,' he told me, 'she hardly ever speaks to a soul now. She won't play with any of her friends and she does no work for the teacher at the school.'

My heart went out to her the minute I set eyes on her. She had these big dark, sad-looking brown eyes, and golden curls, beautiful they were, hanging right down past her shoulders. And she had the loveliest wee face you could picture, pretty as anything, and a cute wee dimple right in the middle of her chin. Ach, sure I'll never forget her, the poor wee craythur, and her only eight year old.

I said I could start work right away so he brought me around the house. It was big, seven rooms up the stairs, and it set in its own private grounds. He kept a gardener full time, an old grizzly, grey fellow with a stumpy temper.

I was given the best room in the house, nice and quiet with a big window looking out over the front lawns. I suppose he must have slept there himself before his wife died. It didn't strike me as funny at the time, that he was paying nearly twice the usual wage for that kind of work. I was only too glad of it, with me saving up to get married and him away in England doing the same.

I was my own boss and didn't have a lot to do. Another woman came in for a couple of hours every morning, and she done the bulk of the cleaning and cooked the dinner. All I had to do really was make the breakfast, and the tea in the evenings, and get the three young ones out to school. And sure it was nothing, working in a house like that with all them mod-cons. I spent a lot of time with Jean, playing with her and reading her wee stories to try to take her out of herself. I had plenty of time on me hands so I used to go down to the school at lunchtimes to see if she was alright. And God, the way her wee face used to light up whenever she seen me coming, it would have done your heart good. People were soon saying what a great change they seen in her since I come. One day the teacher came out and shaked my hand and said I was a godsend, a real godsend.

I was working there for around three months before I found out what was going on. I took a bad dose of the flu and I had to get up in the middle of the night, a thing I didn't usually do. In them days I was a great sleeper. The bathroom was at the back of the house, where the family slept. It was two o'clock in the morning, I can still mind well looking at my luminous alarm-clock when I woke up in a cold sweat. I didn't bother about me slippers or dressing gown but just padded out onto the thick-carpeted landing in me bare feet and nightdress. I had just shut the bathroom door behind me, silently, so as not to waken anybody else at that unearthly hour, when I thought I heard a sob. Sound as you know, has an unnatural way of carrying in the stillness of the night, so I took two aspirins and a long drink of cold water and thought no more about it. I was well up the landing, heading for my own room, when I heard the sound again. It was clearer this time, a sob and a muffled kind of a cry. Something was the matter with Jean. I went straight for her room, and as I groped about in the dark for her light switch, I called out to reassure her, 'It's alright pet, you're only having a nasty old dream.'

My first impression when I switched the light on was that he had got to her first. That impression didn't last long. He was crouched over her naked wee body holding her legs apart with his hands and his pyjamas were lying in an untidy heap on top of her favourite doll.

When I realized what he was doing I rushed over screaming to try to help her. I can't mine what happened next. I must have fainted with the shock and the flu, I suppose. When I came round I was back in my own bed with him sitting there beside me. He had his pyjamas back on again.

The flu I had got a lot worse and my temperature went up shocking high. For a few days I thought I was going to die, but he wouldn't get me a doctor. He took time off his work to take care of me himself. Imagine. Sometimes I thought it was a terrible nightmare, and that I would wake up, only I didn't. It was real.

He wouldn't even let the woman that done the cleaning into me room. He just kept coming in himself and sitting on the bed and me lying there hardly able to move. He kept on saying over and over, 'You won't tell, now will you? Promise me that you won't tell.'

I knew he was mad so I had to promise, just to humour him. I knew too, that with both my parents dead and him away in England, nobody was likely to miss me for a while. I was very much at his mercy.

'I'm a lonely man, a lonely man, a very lonely man,' he kept saying. 'I wouldn't hurt her, I wouldn't hurt her for all the world, she's my own, my very own wee girl.'

After a few days of this he started holding my hand when he was talking. I was too scared at this stage to do anything about it. The strangest look came over his eyes when he started poking at me. I didn't know what he was doing or what was going on when his affair went all stiff. I didn't know that happened to men. I thought it would kill me when he started to jab it into me. I screamed and then passed out with the pain. When I came to he was still at it, shoving his affair into me then nearly pulling it out and shoving it in harder still. He had a mad look on his face when he was doing it and the slevvers were dripping out of his mouth onto my face.

I started to pray to Our Lady to save me. The pain was so bad I could hardly stand it. He kept doing it to me every day till I was near demented. I often think that if it hadn't been for the prayers I would have gone clean mad. It was eight days after he first done it to me that I finally managed to escape. Some businessman called at the house and the cleaning woman let him in and he left in a hurry and forgot to lock my door. Thank God I had enough of my strength left to be up and gone before he came back. It's amazing how quick you can recover when you're young.

I had just enough time to get my few wee pounds out from under my mattress but no time to pack my things. I was in a terrible state about leaving Jean behind. I didn't know right what to do for her so I went straight away to the Redemptorists on the Antrim Road. They're very powerful men the Redemptorists. I've always had great faith in them. The priest I talked to was very nice. He couldn't have been nicer, and he was more than understanding when I went to confession. He said there was no way any blame could be attached to me. I was completely innocent of any sin. He said I was very close to God and he made me promise in confession that I would never go near that house again. He asked me would I talk to him outside confession about it and I said I would. He took the name and address and said that he would see to it that wee Jean would be alright. Then he told me to pray for the man because he was evil. Indeed I still pray for him even though he's bound to be dead now, for that was a long time ago.

Well, to make a long story short, I might as well tell you, it all kept playing on my mind. I had nobody to talk to with my mother dead so I kept on brooding about it in my head and worrying over what had become of poor wee Jean. I know now that I made a mistake. I shouldn't have told him a thing about it when he came home from England that Christmas, but as I say, it kept playing on my mind and I needed somebody to talk to.

The priest had told me that I was still a virgin in the eyes of God and his church, but when I told him what happened, he said he didn't want to marry a woman that wasn't pure. I never got over that right. I've been in and out of places like this ever since, especially at this time of year. You know, I thought I could depend on him. After all I had been through. I never thought he could view it like that. That was the last thing I thought.

The Godmother

'**A** come on mammy, let hir go. Let me tek hir, a'm hir Godmother.' Martha, the mother, is standing at the big black range that dominates the room, stirring a pot of porridge.

'Ye needn't remind me that ye'r hir Godmother, a know it well inoff, you goin' away an' callin' hir Barbara, when ye knew a wanted hir called after yer aunt Maggie. A shouldn't hev let ye talk me inte lettin' you stan' for hir anyway, an' you takin' hir away te the chapel way them big black gloves up te yer elbows, a knew when a seen ye comin' in the gate that it would bring bad luck, an' now ye want te tek hir out agen.'

'For Christ's sake, ma, that wos four years ago, are ye aff yer head? A only want te tek hir te Derry for a day out.'

Martha still stirs the porridge that she calls brochan with the stubborn back of her head turned towards her eldest daughter, Sarah.

'Get outa me sight an' don't let me hear another word about it,' she says.

Sarah, determined Godmother that she is, hasn't finished yet.

'Ma, de ye want hir te en' up lek me? At fourteen years a age a hadn't been out the foot a the town. A don't want Barbara te be so gullible. A niver toul ye this before, but a think a better tell ye now. De ye mine the time our Kate was born?'

Martha swings round dangerously with the saucepan of porridge in her hand and heads towards the door.

'De ye mine the time our Kate wos born – huh – as if a'm

lekely te forget that. The ol' rubbish you talk. Fit ye better ye would clean up that house. A do'no how a iver managed te rear a wan lek ye.'

Sarah rushes after her out into the yard.

'Please listen te me ma, it's important. De ye mine when our Kate wos born an' a went up te Altnagalvin Hospital te tek ye home in a taxi? It wos Paddy Doherty's taxi, an' a wos sittin' up in the front seat beside him.'

Martha's head suddenly jerks forward and she peers at Sarah suspiciously. 'Well, come on, out way it, what did the ol' bugger do? Why hev ye waited all this time te tell me?'

She grabs Sarah and pushes her inside and onto a chair.

'Right me lady, let's hear it all. Jest wait till a tell yer da. He'll hev somethin' te say te ye for keepin' quiet about it all these years. Now, start at the beginnin', an' lave nothin' out, mine. Ye wor sittin' up in the front seat beside him?'

'Alright, alight, calm down, calm down, don't get hysterical, ma. A do'no what has caused the sudden interest, a wheen a minutes ago ye didn't want te hear another word outa me.'

Martha stretches herself to her full four foot ten inches, puts her hands on her haunches and stands before her daughter, waiting, a woman with a grievance.

'A wos sittin' up in the front seat beside him,' Sarah repeats, 'an' we wor goin' out the foot a the town, now a didn't know where a wos, because a had niver been out the foot a the town before.'

'So he parked the car,' says Martha, glaring at her.

'Now what would he want te do that for mammy? We wor headin' for Derry.'

'Don't act innocent way me me lady, a know the kine a man he is.'

'Well a'm glad ye do,' says Sarah, 'a know the kine a man he is too, he's good an' generous an' kind, in fact, he's the kindest man a iver met.'

'O Sacred Heart of Jesus,' says Martha, making the sign of the cross and beating her breast, 'what kine of a rearin' is this? A'll hev te go an' get Father Curry. How am a goin' te tell him. How am a goin' te tell him, an' him a walkin' saint.'

'Ye won't let me finish, will ye mother? Ye don't know what he done.'

'Ye dirty rotten bitch,' screams Martha, 'a know very well what he done.'

'What the hell's the point in me tryin' te tell you anythin', ye hev already decided that ye know what happened.'

'A noticed a change in ye, a wondered what it wos, now a know, now a know. God help me, a know now.'

Sarah, jumping up from her chair, grabs her mother by the shoulders, shakes her, and implores her to listen.

'Ma, he didn't do anythin' bad or wrong, honest.'

'Ye don't know the difference between right an' wrong, an' a brought ye up to be a good catholic girl. Didn't do anythin' wrong, ye poor girl, are ye simple?'

'No, a'm not simple, ma, but a must be mad, tryin' te explain anythin' te you.'

'Don't talk back te yer mother,' says Martha. 'This ol' bastard an' you are goin' out the bottom a the town, then what happens, get on way yer story.'

'Will ye stap callin' him an ol' bastard,' yells Sarah, 'when a toul ye afore that he's not.'

'Holy Mother of Jesus look down on me this day, te think that it hes come te this,' Martha drops to the floor, to her knees, with her eyes upturned.

'Don't, mother, please', pleads Sarah, but to no avail, Martha is too far gone. She jumps to her feet and rushes to the back of the door where her old green coat is hanging from a nail.

'A'm goin' te see Father Curry, now, this very minute. A'm gettin' him here te hear yer confession.'

'Ye'r doin' nothin' a the kine. The days are past when a would go te confession te that ol' pervert. A've had inoff a him. If ye'r lookin' for a likely candidate for the title 'dirty bastard' ye hev yer man now alright.'

Martha grabs a bottle of holy water from the windowsill and starts to sprinkle it all over Sarah, thinking, that perhaps the holy water will succeed where her prayers failed. Sarah snatches the bottle from her hand and hurls it to the floor.

'Get yer holy water outa me sight an' listen te me for a change. There's a few things ye want te know about yer friend Father Curry. De ye happen te be aware that he is responsible for corruptin' half the innocent wains in the parish wi hes lurid suggestions in confession? The lucky wans get confession over in the confessional box. They're not told that their sins are so unspeakable, as to require special attention in the parochial house.'

Martha is now pale and speechless. Taking advantage of the lull, Sarah begins to imitate the slow drawl of the old priest's voice:

'Sit up close to me, wee girl, are you cold, child, let me feel, are you cold? You have committed some very grave sins, child. Isn't that right? Now tell me about them. Do you touch your wee body, child? Now don't be afraid. Come closer. Close your eyes, child. Nothing to be afraid of, child. You're a nice wee child, aren't you? Do you let wee boys look at you? At your wee body, child? Good, good don't be afraid...'

Martha is fingering her prayer beads now with her eyes closed tight. 'Hev ye finished way this blasphemy?' asks her mother, calmer now after her prayers.

'No, mother, as a wos sayin' before, a wos sittin' up in the front seat beside him an' we wor goin' out the foot a the town but a didn't know where a wos because a had niver been out the foot a the town before. Now he didn't park the car as we wor headin' for Derry – understand mother? A sed te him after a wheen a minutes, is that the hospital up there? No, he sed back te me, it's not, that's Joe Henry's creamery. O, says a te him, we get our milk from Joe. That's right, says he, now ye know where it comes from. We drove on, mother, an' a asked him a lot a other gullible questions. He answered them but eventually he asked, what age are you lassie? A sed fourteen. Then he sed, hev ye iver been in Derry before? A sed, no. Then he sed, fourteen, an' ye've niver been te Derry. He looked sad, ma. Then he started te tell me as we drove along, te save me the bother a askin' questions, the names a the people who lived here an' there an' what had happened at the various places.

After a while we come te the lights at Altnagelvin Hospital. He wos about te turn in when he stapped an' sed te me, now lassie, yer ma is alright up there, she's in hir bed, warm an' snug, they're not goin' te throw hir out. A'm tekin' ye to Derry. A wouldn't hev it on me conscience that a tuk ye this close without bringin' ye te see it. He tuk me up te Derry ma. He showed me the River Foyle an' he showed me the Guildhall an' he tuk me up onte the wall te look at the 'Roarin' Meg'. He brought me te the Bogside, the Brandywell an' St. Columb's Wells. He showed me St. Eugene's Cathedral an' the *Derry Journal* offices. He bought me an ice-cream, mammy, an' a bottle a Coca-Cola an' when we wor comin' over the bridge on the way out, he sed te me, "Now lassie, ye can niver say ye havn't been te Derry."

A didn't tell ye, ma, because a know ye – an' – a wos – a wos – a wos feard.'

The man of the house

'Don't send him, mammy. If you let him stay I'll be good, I'll never be bad again. I'll bring in the coal and turf and wash the dishes and make the beds and do all the washing and everything, but please, don't let him go. I'll kneel up nice and straight and never make faces when the rosary is on. I'll dig the hole and empty the bucket and wash out the lavatory every day. When I go to granny's for the buttermilk I won't stop again at the river. I'll be good, wil' good, all the time, honest ma, but please, please, don't let him go.'

'It's too late, he's going. I can't look after him and all you lot as well, with your da away in jail, so go away and don't bother me.'

'But, ma, you could ask daddy to come home, he only has to sign himself out, like uncle Pat done'.

'Don't mention that name in this house. Your uncle Pat, a nice Irishman he turned out to be – signing himself out. I never thought I'd live to see the day. How dare you suggest that your father would do such a thing. Nobody ever asked him to sign himself in.'

'But, ma, he said he'd never stay in against your wishes, that all you had to do was say the word. If he signed himself out, our wee Mark could stay at home, he wouldn't have to go away. Gone and ask him, please, mammy, and I'll be good I tell you, I'll be good, wil' good, all the time.'

'You've been reading my letters again, you wee bugger you. I thought I told you before about that. I'll get your Uncle

Bill to give you a good lacing if you don't mend your ways.'

'I'm not feared of him. If he lays one finger on me he'll be sorry. I'll get my da to give him a quare good hiding when he comes home. My da isn't one bit feared of your weird old bachelor brother. My da would break his oul' face for him.'

'Your da would give you a good beating himself if he heard you now, me boy. You have a lot of notions in your head about him, he's been too long away.'

'Well, you could get him out you know, all you have to do is say the word.'

'Get him out indeed! He would like that. Then he'd be able to say that the wife asked him. I tell you, I'm not that soft, he'll stay where he is till they let him out. They'll not say I didn't do my bit for the cause, indeed they'll not.'

'But what will happen to wee Mark, away on his own among strangers? He'll be so lonely.'

'Don't be silly, he wouldn't know to be lonely. He'll be better looked after there than he is at home with all them nurses and doctors. And what's more, your da agreed with me, so I'll hear no more about it.'

'Well I think it's mean sending him away when he's one of the family. He should live here with us.'

'He knows nothin' about things like families. He'd be happy anywhere he was fed and washed and looked after. That's what these places are for, people like him. Father Curry told me that he'll never be right. He says it's God's will and the sooner we get him into one of these places the better. Who do you think you are to argue with the priest?'

'He's not the priest's brother, he's mine and you didn't ask me. You didn't ask any of us. Our Joan doesn't want him to go either. Ask her, go on, ask her, ma.'

'Do you think I'm uneasy about what our Joan thinks? Now get out of my road I've a lot of things to get ready for the morrow.'

'I'm not going to school the morrow. I'm staying here. I'm not letting them take him. Me and our Joan are staying here and locking up the door.'

'That's right,' Joan said, 'We're not letting any old ambulance take our wee Mark away to no old hospital.'

'I make the decisions round here. He's goin' tomorrow, and that's the end of it. You two'll go to school like any other day.'

'We'll not, you know,' they answered firmly. But next morning found them trudging down the long grey lane, crying. 'We'll never see him again. He's going. They're taking him away.'

They arrived in school, late as usual. The teacher called them as they came in.

'Never able to make it on time, you two idlers. Come up here to the front, the pair of you. Mary Kelly, for the benefit of these two, would you mind repeating the last question?'

'Yes miss, "Wherein consists the love we owe our neighbour?", miss.'

'That's right Mary, thank you Mary. Joan?'

'Don't know, miss.'

'I suppose the big brother doesn't know either.'

'No, miss.'

'Mary, would you be so kind?'

'Yes, miss. "In being full of goodwill towards him", miss,' "and in doing nothing unto him, that we would not have done unto ourselves", miss.'

'Thank you, Mary dear. Now if you two would only take a leaf out of Mary's book.'

'If that's what you want us to do Miss, we will, and gladly,' he said with abandon, bounding towards Mary's desk and grabbing her catechism. He ripped a page from it and offered it to his sister, inviting her to do the same. Fear prevented her. He was past caring.

'Now if you'll excuse me, miss, I've got things to do,' he said and headed for the door. His sister followed.

Outside, running madly in the direction of home, he yelled to her over his shoulder,' I'm the man of the house now. They're not taking him. Hurry or we might be late.'

They were. She knew when she saw the ambulance turning

out of the end of the lane. He had stopped pulling his hair out when she got to him, an old man of eleven, standing stooped in the lane, inarticulate, capable only of a stutter. 'T - T - Th - The - They - t - t - to - too - took - h - h - hi - him'.

Later, after he had dragged himself home, he was consumed by a terrible fury which raged for a full five minutes, breaking everything in its wake. When all the delph was smashed he started on the cutlery, clamping spoons and forks tight in his hands and bending them till the veins stood out in his neck. Then the tears came.

When his mother discovered what he had done she rushed off across the fields, screaming for aid from her brother Bill. He was only too willing to assist.

'That's right, take the trousers off him,' his mother urged, 'he has my heart broke. Lay on him. Lay on him. Give him a good trounsing.'

'Don't you worry, I'll make him sorry for his carry-on the longest day he ever lives.'

The buckle of the belt inflicted most pain. Round and round in a circle they went, the blood-stained buckle flashing in the firelight. When it was over, he crawled whimpering into a corner.

'And let that be a lesson to the rest of you,' thundered the uncle in triumph. 'He'll mind this day. I mark you. You'll have no more bother with that boy now.'

A bee in a bottle

'If you listen out right you'll hear me at a quarter to six, driving up Jack Long's brae coming home, like a bee in a bottle,' he used to tell us.

He drove a Norton 250, and sometimes when it didn't reply to his kick starts at a quarter to seven in the morning, we'd fight each other for the privilege of pushing him all the way to the end of the road.

You could set your clock by his comings and goings. At a quarter to six the mild drone of a bee would begin. He'd just be starting to climb Jack Long's brae, and the further up the brae he got, the more furiously the bike buzzed, sounding as if it really was a bee inside a bottle. Sound echoed far, trapped in the Sperrin Mountains. It would be another fifteen minutes before he'd appear at the gate. We thought he looked very distinguished, dressed in his working clothes, with his cap on backways and his goggles.

He always changed his clothes and washed with carbolic soap in a basin of cold water before sitting down to dinner. Ate everything put before him, and after, made the sign of the cross always, and said, 'That was nice, Maggie.' Then he would tell her the news. What he had done that day. Who he had met. What they had said to him. What he had said back to them. How they were looking, poor creathures. What was happening to them all. Who had to have operations. Who had a stroke of good luck. The latest report on some old folk. How people's children were getting along. Who had emigrated. Who had got a job. The births. The marriages. The deaths. He was a talking evening newspaper.

After the news he would tell us a story. Maybe it would be about a mischievious leprechaun that had wreaked havoc up in Park. Or it might be about a donkey he talked to down near the Salmon Leap. A donkey that stood looking out over a gate. The same donkey that had surprised him, half scared him out of his wits one day by shouting after him in an old craggy voice, 'Are you the man with the houseful of nice fair-haired wee wains that lives out the mountain road?' His caution on approaching the donkey, looking around nervously to make sure that nobody else was watching, in case they thought he was crazy for talking to it. The donkey's interest in us all. The donkey's knowledge. 'Was Tish's sore throat getting any better? Was the hair starting to grow back on the bald patch that the ring-worm left on Pascal's head? Had Breige got the money the tooth fairy left for her out at the back door? Was the cut Gerard got on his finger healed yet? Was Ann getting any fatter. He worried that there wasn't a pick on her. Did Michael ever do a bloody thing but read?' Then he'd distribute the sweets and penny chews that the donkey had told him to get us. We wrote letters to the donkey. The donkey wrote back.

He was a bin-man. On a Friday he didn't need his Norton, for the bin-lorry came to our town instead. That was the day we got the prog. Our favourite day of the week. Prog was the name we had for things other people threw away that were far too good to be dumped. Most of the clothes we wore were prog. First they had to be disinfected and washed and ironed. Then we'd parade around in them to be inspected, feeling as regal as royalty at Ascot.

'Mother of God! The things that people throw out'

'When you think of all the starvation in the world, it would make you sad'

'It's hard to credit, isn't it?'

'Imagine!'

'God have mercy on us anyway!'

We'd stand around in a semi-circle, wide-eyed with wonder, while he fished each individual item from the prog-bag, telling the story about the place it came from. The English airmen's wives at Ballykelly aerodrome threw out the best stuff. What kind of money these people were making, to have so much to throw away, could only be guessed at.

A doctor's wife in Limavady didn't throw good things into her dustbin. One day she came out and asked him if any of the clothes her children had grown out of would be of use to his wife? She said she hoped she wasn't offending him. It would be a sin to allow them to waste.

'A lovely woman.'

The things from the doctor's wife didn't need washing. She always put them out, separate from the rubbish, clean and freshly laundered in a cardboard box. She must have had a daughter a year or two older than me, or an inch or two taller, for I was often the beneficiary of some stylish coats and frocks.

He cut the best turf on Toner's bog (though some may dispute this), and it was there one day, while working turf, when I was long gone from home, that he had his first stroke. They didn't write to tell me at the time:

'No point in bothering her.'

'We'll wait and see if he gets any better first.'

'It would only worry her.'

'She has enough troubles of her own.'

'And tell me, what could she do anyway?'

'Ach, sure he's doing great now. He's as right as rain again, he is.'

'Leave it, she'll find out soon enough, the creathure.'

He couldn't lift dustbins after that. They gave him a job sweeping streets. He was fifty-five. When I saw him again, I mistook him for Uncle Frank. My favourite uncle, luckily, but his older brother. His much older brother.

Time passed. More strokes. Other visits. Last time, finally.

I was taken to a strange man in a hospital bed, and accepting it was him, said, 'Hello daddy.'

The nurse had made a mistake. So had I.

I cannot go to see him anymore. Cannot face that stranger sitting there. Cannot face his sad unseeing eyes. Cannot face the changes wrought by three savage strokes.

I'm afraid of what it will do to me. Afraid of what it will take from me. I need to keep him alive. Need to hear his stories in my head. Need to remember Fridays waiting eagerly for prog. Need to remember his bright blue eyes, telling my mother the news. Telling us all how he talked to a donkey.

But most of all, I need to close my eyes of an evening, and listen for him, driving up Jack Long's brae, coming home at a quarter to six on his Norton 250, sounding just for all the world, like a bee in a bottle.

The fortune teller

Catherine had no idea where she was going. Left to herself, she would still be in her room counting the floral patterns on the wall opposite her bed. From top to bottom on the side near the door, were twenty seven faded roses. From left to right along the bottom, forty and two bits. The two bits irked her. The first bit was squashed between the second and third sheets where the wallpaper overlapped.

Her father had hung that paper when they had all lived together. As a small girl she fancied that he had had some mysterious reason for concealing a part of that rose. Later, when the family split up and plans were afoot to redecorate the whole house, she had kicked up such a fuss that her mother had, in the end, decided to leave her room as it was.

The other spare bit was sliced clean in half where the wallpaper met the paint at the angle with the corner. She had never liked that corner, as the flaw was repeated, each time in slightly extending ascent, till it reached the eleventh row where the pattern was perfect, but only at that one point. The eleventh hour reprieve, she called it, for it started to diminish on the twelfth line. That eleventh row of flowers had always been her favourite in the days when her father's overlap had held mystery for her, but nowadays it made her sad, in a manner she could not fully understand.

Her mother brought her in a third cup of coffee, and finally coaxed her out of bed.

Her mother was great at pretending. Her mother pretended

to worry about nothing. Her mother worried about everything. She worried about things most people had never heard of. When Farming Today announced the birth of the first genetically engineered calf to carry a human gene, Catherine's mother was ill for a week and pretended that she had the flu. She pretended not to worry about Catherine when she sat in her room for three days, looking at the wall, following the break-up with her boyfriend. It was Catherine herself who had made the break, and she was feeling very pleased to be free of him. Still, her mother worried Catherine out of her bed and out of the house. That's why she found herself, with her mother's last five pound note in her pocket, going no place in particular.

She walked along till she reached the gap in the promenade where the recently extracted Derby Baths should have been. No chance of going for a swim there again. Catherine waited for the Fleetwood tram to pass. She felt for the lucky penny which she always carried in her pocket and turned it over, allowing it as ever to decide for her. 'Heads, right, tails, left.' She drew her hand slowly from her pocket and opened her palm. The Queen's head was facing down. The coin had been minted in the year Catherine was born, 1974.

She put the penny back in her pocket and looked away across the muddy sand. Small children with buckets and spades were digging or building castles. Others were paddling, splashing and swimming. Children from out of town enjoying a day by the seaside.

Catherine followed the slopes that led to the lower promenade and turned south in obedience to the coin. She slowed to a stop then and sat on a siding so as not to disturb a nervous flapping pigeon, struggling with a too-large crust of bread which it finally lost to a gull.

The pavements were crowded and filled with voices.

'Mum, yer promised.'

'Shur up.'

'But mum...'

'Shur yer f...ing gob.'

The laughter of day-tripping teenagers was sharp and jarring. She felt excluded, not just for then, but for always.

She wanted to return to the solitude of her room but her mother's worry won. Better stop out a little longer. She could not pretend to have had a good time so quickly. She forced herself to walk faster. The Royal York Hotel was decked out with plastic flags from several countries. After the flags came flowers. A grotesque pansy with angry bulging eyes glared at her from a lamp standard on Leinster Parade. It seemed to guard the entrance to a fortune teller's booth beneath. Catherine crossed the road to read the gipsy's details. A direct descendant of an old Romany family, the sign proclaimed, not make-believe but the real thing. Inside the gipsy was watching a chat show on a tiny television.

'What is make believe,' Catherine wondered, 'what is the real thing?' She moved on past a pink, pouting tulip, a grinning daffodil, a cankerous sunflower and a rude, repulsive rosebud protruding from a monstrous stalk. A middle-aged woman stepped into her path. 'John Lennon is dead,' the woman said, 'John Lennon is dead. He copped it.' The woman reminded her of her mother. She searched the faces of passers-by, hoping to find a happy one but was disappointed. Only two elderly nuns, walking arm in arm, in blue habits, one speaking earnestly, the other listening eagerly, both with enraptured, animated expressions, gave her room for hope.

Advertisements screamed of bargains heaped on bargains from every available inch of pavement. Then her eyes focussed on a picture of a knowing, posing child with a tear drenched face, framed above the caption, 'Why God Likes Little Girls'.

'Oh please, no more, please,' she said almost aloud and moved off the front at the next turning. As she rounded the corner an ice-cream cone flew through the air from a group of boys across the road and splattered the front of a lady's dress to rousing cheers from the lads. The lady was very old. Catherine felt in her pocket for a hankie and helped her out of the firing line. She was eighty-six years old and had been coming to Blackpool every June, to the same hotel, for over forty years. Reared five children and had now nine grandchildren and six great-grandchildren. Blackpool folk were the friendliest folk you could meet. Knew how to make strangers welcome. But things were changing. The young were completely out of control. The police couldn't do nothing, what with social workers interfering and sticking their noses in. The teachers in the schools couldn't lay a finger on them. There was no religion anymore. It was the sixties that was to blame. Hippies. The permissive society. Decent standards needed bringing back. Maggie was doing her best but her hands were tied.

Catherine nodded to all that was said and with every nod her mind grew more confused. When she and the lady finally parted Catherine found herself standing dazed, staring at a photograph of the Princess of Wales before she had become the Princess of Wales. She was about to turn aside when a coarse female voice at her ear said in a strong local accent, 'Come in and talk to me, dear.' The face's owner was holding back a beaded curtain and beckoning Catherine into a very small booth. Claustrophobia almost strangled the girl as she was manoeuvred onto a seat by the large, imposing 'world famous gipsy'.

'What age are you, dear?' the woman asked, getting to the point without ceremony.

'Sixteen,' Catherine told her reluctantly.

'You take things very much to heart,' the gipsy observed, 'Do you follow my meaning, dear?'

'Yes,' Catherine muttered.

'You have things on your mind. Do you have a boyfriend?'

'Yes. No.' Catherine felt annoyance at this invasion of her privacy. She wished to be away. She stood to leave but the woman stayed her with a heavily ringed hand.

'Don't be afraid, dear. I am your friend. Let me read your palm. I can guide you.'

When the gipsy took hold of Catherine's left wrist, she felt herself shudder again. The woman peered at the lines on the girl's hand.

'Many things are going to happen in your future life,' the gipsy predicted. 'I can give you good advice. I can help you. Just cross my hand with silver.'

'I have no silver,' Catherine confessed, all I have is a five pound note.'

'Five pounds is okay, it doesn't have to be silver.' The gipsy's eyes were lifeless as stone. Catherine put her hand into her pocket and handed over the five pound note. The woman stroked the money across the girl's palm and gave a hasty recitation of her future. Marriage to a handsome, successful man, two beautiful children, a boy and a girl, fabulous wealth, foreign travel, no serious health problems, a very long and happy life. Before she had time to catch her breath, Catherine found herself being bundled out through the beaded curtain, back on to the pavement.

She stood still to take stock of what had happened. She had been robbed and there was nothing she could do about it. She suppressed a strong urge to cry. She wanted to run home to be consoled but decided not to. She knew what her mother would say anyhow. She could almost hear her words. 'You really should not feel that way, darling, of course you are not stupid. Advantage takers are the real losers, for they rob themselves of their own humanity.'

Catherine felt that she had been pushed to the verge of a different world. She attempted to fit the events of the day together in her mind but they stayed jumbled. If her lucky penny had turned up 'heads' would she now be a different person? She would certainly have gone on a pleasanter walk. Met different people. Might even have returned to the safety of her room to count the faded flowers. Flower power. She imagined the beautiful, vacant John Lennon woman, young and with her mother as a girl. Yes, that was what she and her mother had in common, they had both grown up in the sixties. And, if she had not offered help to the frail old woman would she still have fallen within the fortune teller's grasp? She drew comfort from the thought that the greedy gipsy woman was much too old to have grown up in the sixties.

Out of habit, she turned the lucky penny over in her pocket. She took it out and opened her palm, it had come up 'heads'. But this time she had asked for no directions. She stepped closer to the beaded curtain, hesitating, unsure whether or where to knock when the richly ringed hand drew it apart. 'Do you want a reading, dear?'

'What do you want now?' she rasped, sounding like the dreaded Marina who served cold dinners in the school canteen, a challenge rather than a question, 'I've already done you.'

'I know you have,' Catherine said, 'and I'm sorry. I just want to give you something. It's my lucky penny.' She placed the coin on the gipsy's palm and looked into the hard eyes. She felt the last vista of childhood recede behind her.

The devil's gift

Harry Ryan sat sullenly in a big wooden chair at the top of the table.

Mary, his wife, an ample woman of forty, was dishing out food. John, their son, tried to lend an air of good humour to the whole procedure, while his sister, Clair, helped serve up. Harry didn't keep them in suspense for very long.

'Well, Holy Christ!' he started, addressing no-one in particular, 'I thought I'd heard it all, but a nun, our fine lady a nun!'

John pulled his chair closer to the table and clenched his teeth.

Harry repeated the taunt, 'A nun, a nun, our fine lady, a nun!'

Mary threw a listless look at him across the table. 'I thought I asked you to leave her alone,' she said, 'Haven't you been at her long enough?'

'Long enough. Long enough,' he mimicked, 'Don't long enough me woman. Heading off to become a bloody nun, just when she's old enough to earn a bit of money.'

His wife only argued with a sigh, absently changing the baby from one breast to the other.

'Listen to yourself,' John shouted, pushing his chair away from the table in disgust. 'If you'd ever learned to keep your trap shut, Clair might not be running off to throw her life away. She thinks all men are like you, and could you blame her?'

The younger children made a quick retreat under the table when their father rose to his feet. He drove his knife into the table.

'You see the kind of a rearing you have there, woman?' Harry roared at his wife. But amazingly, there were no fireworks. Harry just grabbed his coat from the back of his chair and stormed out, banging the door behind him.

At nine o'clock next morning when she'd closed the door on the last straggler off to school, Mary sighed.

'Thank God,' she said to Clair, 'Now we can have a cup of tea to ourselves before we start cleaning.' The room was its usual early morning mess, shoes and dirty clothes strewn about the floor, bulging cupboards hanging open exposing every imaginable kind of junk.

Clair wet the tea and made space for two cups on a corner of the table. Mary continued talking.

'It'll take them the best part of four hours to drive from Athgar. Just as well too, with the work we have to do. And don't forget, as soon as we have the house cleaned, you need to wash and change into your new frock. You look like a scarecrow.'

'Well', Clair said, laughing, as she started to pour the tea, 'Look who's talking!' As she spoke she nearly dropped the tea pot. Two nuns were opening the gate, their habits flapping vigorously in the wind.

'Mammy, they're here, the nuns,' she gasped.

Mary jerked to her feet. 'Holy mother of God, what are we going to do?' she asked. 'We can't bring them into a house like this, and we can't leave them standing on the doorstep.'

Mary dashed towards the back bedroom. 'I can't see them. Tell them I'm sick,' she said.

'Mammy, please don't,' Clair pleaded. 'If they think you're ill, they won't take me.'

They made a frantic effort to tidy the place, opening the bedroom door and pitching armfuls of clothes and shoes out of sight. The knocking grew persistent.

'We'll have to let them in now,' Mary whispered. 'You go, Clair.'

'No, mammy, please, you go.'

In the end they went to the door together, one looking as flustered and embarrassed as the other. On the doorstep stood two women, dressed in the habit of Francis of Assisi.

The oldest of the pair, a frail woman of fifty, spoke first. 'Mrs Ryan? I'm Reverend Mother Virtue, and this is Sister Veronica, our directress of vocations.'

'I'm pleased to meet yous both. This is Clair.'

Clair opened her mouth to speak but when no sound came she closed it again and lowered her head.

'Oh dear, I've forgotten my manners, won't yous come in?' said Mary. A picture of Jesus, his heart exposed and bleeding, watched impassively from a vantage point high up on a wall above a votive light, flanked by jam jars packed with wild flowers and with evergreens from the hedgerows thereabout.

'Yous'll excuse the state of the house I hope, the wains has just gone to school,' Mary continued, clearing armfuls of soiled clothes from two chairs. Both nuns continued to stand.

'Would you like a cup of tea, reverent mother?'

'No, thank you, Mrs Ryan.'

'How about you, Sister?'

'Thank you, Mrs Ryan, you are most kind,' she answered with a half smile.

'How many children do you have, Mrs Ryan?' the reverend mother enquired as she examined her surroundings.

'Ten.'

'Is Clair the eldest?'

Clair felt her heart leap, this was the first time her presence had been acknowledged.

'No, reverent mother, she's not, I have a boy, John, one year older.'

The nuns sat down.

'So you think you have a vocation in the religious life, Clair?'

'Yes, reverent mother.' She faltered then added almost inaudibly, 'Well, I think so, reverent mother.'

'Do you think you will be able to study, Clair?' Sister Veronica asked. 'I understand from your letter that you have little schooling.'

'I didn't get a lot of schooling, sister,' she blurted out, 'but I've always wanted to learn more.'

'Good, very good,' Sister Veronica smiled, 'God expects us all to try our hardest, Clair.'

'What kind of work does your husband do, Mrs Ryan?' the reverend mother enquired.

'Well, you see,' Mary began, stalling, 'there has never been a lot of work around here for catholic men. Mind you, he takes anything that comes up, he's a good worker and never likes to be idle. For the past few weeks,' she added, her confidence growing 'he's been working on my father's farm.'

'Your father is a farmer, Mrs Ryan?' the reverend mother said.

'Indeed he is,' Mary bragged 'all the land to the road belongs to my father.'

Clair, smarting with mortification, began sweeping the range.

'You see that machinery in the big field up there?' Mary said, pointing, 'and them cows, they all belong to my father.'

The nuns exchanged knowing looks.

'Are you depending at all on Clair's future earnings?' the Reverend Mother asked.

'There's no need to be worrying about the like of that, reverent mother,' Mary assured her serenely.

'Very well,' the reverend mother said slowly, casting a slightly deprecatory glance around the room.

'We receive postulants twice a year,' she said. 'On February 2nd and August 15th. Which date is most convenient?'

'February,' Clair replied, heart in her mouth.

'Should you not ask your mother's permission first?' Mother Virtue asked with a smile.

'No, no, it's up to Clair to decide,' Mary broke in, tears choking her voice with the realization of what had been decided.

'Very well. I'll expect you on February 2nd, my child. Now we must be off,' she said, rising. Mary began to rummage through her purse.

'Here's a wee something to help you with the petrol.'

Clair looked on in astonishment as the reverend mother slipped the five pounds into a slit at the side of her habit.

'I'll see that Clair gets something nice with this when she comes to us,' she said.

When the nuns had gone Clair made fresh tea for the two of them and pored over the documents left behind by the reverend mother.

'Are you of legitimate parentage?' Clair shrugged, determined to borrow a dictionary, and read aloud the next question. 'Is there any public stain on the family?'

'Was daddy being in jail a public stain on our family?' Clair asked.

'Clair Ryan,' Mary exploded. 'Your father never appeared in a court in his life. He was dragged out of bed in the middle of the night by 'B' men and thrown into Crumlin Road Jail. I didn't know whether he was alive or dead. Public stain indeed. Stormont is a public stain. In troth, I'll have something to say to these nuns if they try to public stain me.'

'Sorry, ma,' Clair said, gently easing the paper from her grasp. 'Sure wasn't Francis himself locked away.'

'That wouldn't surprise me in the least,' Mary fumed, 'nothing would be low enough for them 'B' men.'

The nun's documents became the focal point of the family's attention over the next few days. Neighbours called in to scrutinise them. The list of personal belongings that Clair was supposed to take with her created the greatest sensation, with everybody clamouring to find out what a nun wore under her habit. Great surprise was expressed that she should need twelve pairs of black stockings. What for, nobody could be sure, except John, who said they'd make a great rope ladder if she wanted to escape. An old lady took Clair aside and put her right. Twelve, she explained, was understood to be the total number of undergarments required. The nuns could not write such words as knickers, brassieres and suspenders, for reasons of refinement and decorum.

As the leaving day approached, a heaviness descended on the family. No voice was raised in anger or in mirth and every precaution was taken never to allude to the coming event. Outside the house, all was friendliness. Everyone wanted to talk to Clair, to shake her hand, to seek her opinion.

Some mothers brought their errant teenage girls along to her, with requests that she put them back on the right path. Why their daughters could not be more like Clair, these mothers could not understand. Mere acquaintances showered her with gifts, with money, and with requests for prayers. Elderly ladies drew her aside and confided their secrets to her. Clair was everybody's favourite. The toast of the town. When February 2nd came round, she had amassed what she considered a huge fortune, seven hundred and eighteen pounds, two shillings and sixpence, to take with her as a dowry.

The journey to the convent was strained and almost silent and took the best part of four hours. In late afternoon they reached their destination two miles outside Athgar. The convent, an imposing gothic country house, stood gaunt and rambling at the end of a tree-lined avenue. Away to the left half hidden by trees, Lough Nellen appeared dead and lifeless, reflecting the heavy February sky.

Her father braked the car abruptly at the first unexpected sight of the house. He leant his head down over the steering wheel for several seconds before speaking. Mary sat beside him mutely, and Clair, watching from the back seat, felt a stab of guilt dart into her. Her parents looked old and defeated.

'Listen pet,' her father faltered, an unfamiliar shake in his voice, 'I've been thinking. Me and your ma, has been thinking,' he corrected himself, looking towards Mary for support, 'And John,' he added hurriedly. 'We've all been thinking, that maybe what you need is a wee holiday. Look, I have the money,' he produced his wallet. 'I got a loan from the Credit Union. How would you like a week in Dublin? We'll see that you get a grand time, and I'll see the people that gave you presents, and give them back myself. I'll explain that we talked you out of going till you were older. What do you say?'

Clair couldn't speak straight away. Her answer never came. They were interrupted by a tapping on the windscreen. A nun, who introduced herself as Sister Mary Patrick, urged them on to the house for fear they should catch their deaths in the cold. That was that.

Mother Virtue greeted them. Clair was sent away down a long corridor with a young nun. She followed, matching her pace to that of the silent figure who walked her through the building, then up a wide staircase. No sound penetrated the thickness of the walls. As they neared the top of a second flight of stairs, Clair was gripped by panic. 'I didn't say goodbye to my parents,' she said in alarm. Have they gone?'

The young nun placed an index finger over her lips before turning silently to mount another flight of stairs. Clair followed quietly, tears brimming.

On the second floor the nun beckoned Clair into an open doorway. 'I couldn't answer your question on the stairs, sister,' she whispered, 'It is a breach of the Holy Rule to speak in any part of the house except the novitiate, and then only during the hour of recreation. In special circumstances it is permitted to speak like this in an open doorway. But not in a corridor or on the stairs. And yes, sister, you will see your parents before they go home. They are in the parlour having tea, but first you must change and go to the refectory for tea.'

They entered a large room. 'This is the postulants' dormitory,' she said. 'Our bed is the one with the curtain drawn around it. On our bed you will find our postulants' garb. Change as quickly as possible. I'll wait for you here.'

'Our bed?' she repeated in astonishment.

'Yes, sister,' the nun replied. 'In the convent we do not have personal possessions. Everything we use, we refer to as ours.'

Her parents left for home an hour later, following a brief reunion. Clair was then introduced to her new companions in a large room on the first floor directly beneath the dormitory. The novitiate was where novices and postulants spent most of their time. Three long tables, positioned edge-to-edge lengthwise, occupied the centre of the floor. A row of bare wooden chairs stood on either side. Facing each other at the opposite ends were two high backed chairs. These belonged to the novice mistress, Mother Peter, and Sister Mary Helen, her assistant.

Mother Peter, a small plump woman with warm brown eyes and a ready smile, had been novice mistress in the house for nearly twenty years and was affectionately referred to as 'our mother'. Sister Mary Helen was large, clumsy and surly and was affectionately referred to by no-one.

'Being the youngest and most junior sister in the house, you must sit beside me, Clair, so that I can keep an eye on you,' the novice mistress told her when the introductions were over.

Seconds later the door opened and Mother Virtue entered.

Everyone in the room bowed reverently saying, as if with only one voice, 'Good evening, reverend mother.'

'Continue, please continue, sisters,' she said, 'let the party commence.'

It was customary in the community to give a welcoming party for new entrants. Clair, as guest, was invited to be seated in the company of Mother Virtue, Mother Peter, and Sister Mary Helen. The entertainment began at once with a choir singing a verse to the tune of Dan O'Hara:

> Now it's here you are today
> In this convent by the lake,
> Even though you may be feeling broken hearted.
> But we soon will chase your gloom
> With our antics round the room,
> And we'll help you to forget
> From whom you've parted.

Then four novices danced a lively hornpipe to music from a record player. Two girls from the Bogside, sisters in real life, sang Greensleeves, a plump young woman with protruding teeth, banged out the Blue Danube on a piano. Every one of forty novices and postulants took her turn. Some sang, some danced, others played instruments, and last of all, a novice called Sister Mary Thelma, recited, in a strong Cork accent, Joseph Mary Plunket's poem, I See His Blood Upon The Rose.

When the frolics finally ended, Clair, very moved by this treat, rose to her feet to thank them and applaud. Clair stopped clapping and sat down quickly. The Reverend Mother spoke to her directly. 'It's your turn now, Clair.'

'But mother, I couldn't.'

'Remember why you are here,' said Mother Virtue. 'It is your turn.'

Overcoming her embarrassment, she recited The Ballad of Peter Gilligan, by W.B. Yeats.

It is well known that the more devout and holy a soul, the more prone it is to temptation from the devil. That in a moment of idleness, the evil one can take possession of an unsuspecting soul and turn even the most fervent around in her tracks, making a complete debauch of her in the twinkling of an eye. So never a moment is spent in idleness in a religious house. So it was in the Franciscan convent of the Holy Angels, Bloomchamp, Athgar.

The day began at half past four in the morning with the ringing of the awakening bell. Each sister, rising from her bed, would say, in answer to the bell, which to her represented the voice of God, *deo gratias*. She would then kiss the floor, an exercise in humility, before washing, dressing, making her bed and hurrying to the chapel for the first prayers of the day. These prayers and mass lasted three hours, and ended with the reverend mother leading the community in single file out of the chapel, chanting psalms, to the refectory for breakfast. Fifteen minutes later, breakfast finished, dishes washed, the same procession would snake its way back to the chapel to give thanks for the gift of food.

The hour between half past eight and nine-thirty was set aside for household chores. It was considered desirable that one should work alone, but where this was not possible, and two or more sisters had to work together, ejaculations were recited aloud and carefully counted so that each nun could later calculate the number of indulgences gained. To the uninitiated, this practice could appear confusing. 'JESUS, one, JESUS, two, JESUS, three, JESUS, four, JESUS, five, JESUS, six, JESUS, seven, JESUS, eight', the sisters would chant in unison as they descended upon a sackful of carrots. Inevitably, as they scraped away, the emphasis would naturally shift to the count, 'ONE THOUSAND THREE HUNDRED AND EIGHTY FOUR, Jesus, ONE THOUSAND THREE HUNDRED AND EIGHTY SIX, Jesus, ONE THOUSAND THREE HUNDRED AND EIGHTY SEVEN, Jesus.'

Between nine-thirty and noon, Monday to Friday, novices and postulants studied. The Angelus bell at mid-day would call the community to prayers before lunch. Twenty minutes were set aside for this, the main meal of the day. Hefty helpings from the Lives of the Saints, depicting scourgings and stonings and every conceivable torture ever inflicted on saintly bishops or holy virgins, would be served with each course to counteract any adverse effects on the spiritual wellbeing of the sisters, derived from too much enjoyment of the food.

Thanksgiving prayers in the chapel followed. Then an hour's preparation for the next day's lessons. A brisk walk in the grounds, then a lesson in deportment.

Choir practice, meditation, stations of the cross and reading from the Holy Office, filled the hours to supper. During this meal, penances for infringements of the Holy Rule were performed publicly in the refectory. An hour's recreation followed. During this hour, sisters were permitted to speak, but only about edifying things. Then private prayers were said in the chapel before all retired for the night at nine-fifteen.

On her first morning Clair was taken aside by Mother Peter

and instructed in the rules and customs of the house. Seating herself behind a desk, the novice mistress ordered Clair to kneel. 'Today,' she intoned gravely when the girl was settled, 'is the first day of a new life for you, Clair. A life dedicated to God. In order to serve God, my dear child, you must practise humility, like our holy father, St Francis. You are now a postulant. Postulant means, begging to be admitted. You are begging to be admitted to the holy order of St Francis. In six months' time, if God wills it, you will be received into the order and given a copy of the Holy Rule by which you will live the rest of your life. As a lay person, you may not read the Holy Rule, but I may quote it to you. And she read: "A sister must, at all times, keep proper custody of the eyes." 'This means that you must at all times keep your eyes downcast. Do not allow them to wander about in the way they did at breakfast this morning.' "A sister must, at all times, keep proper custody of the lips." 'We have a rule of silence, Clair, a strict rule of silence. A sister is never permitted to speak to a companion while alone. She must never discuss her past, her family, or her previous occupation with another.'

'The hours between night prayers and the awakening bell are called the Great Silence.'

'It is absolutely forbidden, except in cases of serious illness, to leave one's bed or to make any sound during the period of the Great Silence.'

"A sister must, at all times, keep proper custody of the hands."

'You must at all times keep your hands under our cape. You must never touch another sister. You must never have a particular friendship. Treat all your sisters in the same way. If you should break a rule, it is your duty to confess it to a superior. If you observe a companion in breach of a rule, it is your duty to report her. You are here to serve God, my child, and to do penance for your sins and the sins of the world.'

The long journey of the previous day followed by a sleepless night had left Clair feeling weak. To add to her discomfort, her period had started unexpectedly early and she had no sanitary towels. She sagged into a more comfortable position, leaning her bottom on the backs of her heels. Mother Peter's voice rose.

'Is that a proper way for a lady to kneel, Clair?' she squeaked, 'You must learn to be a lady before you can be a nun.' Clair knelt up.

'In this community,' Mother Peter continued, 'sisters live by the vows of poverty, chastity, and obedience. With the vow of poverty, sisters give up all rights to personal possessions. Any item brought by you from home, must be placed in the storeroom.'

'With the vow of chastity, sisters give up all rights to personal friendships. You must remove yourself from all human affections, dear child, in order that you may belong entirely to God.'

'With the vow of obedience, sisters give up all rights to personal opinions. From today on, for the rest of your life, you must submit your will, in all humility, to that of your superiors who have been invested with authority from God. Now, Clair, I am giving you a copy of *The Imitation of Christ.* You shall keep your *Imitation* with you at all times and read from it at every opportunity. *The Imitation of Christ* is the bible of the true religious. Only the Christ-fettered are free. You may kiss the floor and go.'

Clair kissed the floor and rose, relieved to find an opening to speak.

'Please mother, can you tell me where to find sanitary towels?'

'Can it wait until after prayers?'

'No mother, I need them now.'

'Then remain here, sister,' Mother Peter said and went out.

Above her desk was a picture showing Francis of Assisi helping Christ down off the cross. She had recently read in a life of St Francis that he was born in the twelfth century. 'That's strange,' she thought.

Mother Peter returned minutes later.

'Here is what you require, sister,' she said, handing a bundle of rags to the girl. 'Take them to our locker now, then go straight to the chapel.'

'What are these?' Clair asked, bewildered.

'These are our sanitary towels, sister.'

'But, but mother...' Clair stuttered.

'They are toweling squares,' Mother Peter explained.

'Wash them after each use in our washing bowl. The one on our locker in the dormitory.'

'The one for washing myself in?'

'Yes, sister. We must keep before our minds the fall of our first mother, Eve. All women who came after her, with the exception of the blessed Virgin Mary, have been tainted by her stain. That stain is God's way of reminding women how corrupt their flesh is, and of warning them never to sin again.'

That evening when the community assembled for supper, Clair lay face down on the centre of the refectory floor with her arms outstretched in cruciform and said aloud in a trembling voice, 'I accuse myself of having spoken disrespectfully to a superior.' Then she got to her knees and crawled from place to place along the line of dining tables, begging a portion of supper from each sister in turn.

Over the next few weeks, Clair grew accustomed to her new way of life. She tried to keep the rules, yet every evening found herself in the centre of the refectory doing public penance. She found an explanation for all her misfortune in Thomas a Kempis' Imitation:

> It is good for us to encounter troubles and adversities from time to time, for trouble often compels a man to search his own heart. It reminds him that he is an exile here, and that he can put trust in nothing in this world. It is good, too, that we sometimes suffer opposition, and that men think ill of us and misjudge us, even when we do and mean well. Such things are an aid to humility, and preserve us from

pride and vainglory. For we more readily turn to
God as our witness, when men despise us and think
no good of us.

Clair committed the passage to memory and redoubled
her efforts to improve. When her superiors misjudged her
after that, she knew it was the will of God.

After six months in the convent her turn came to ring the
bell. This was a major event in the life of a postulant, the
bell's peal representing as it did, the voice of God. Each
postulant took it in weekly turns to ring every bell of the day,
from the awakening bell in the morning, to the final bell at
bedtime.

The most crucial test of any new bell ringer's skill came
on a Friday night when the *De Profundis* bell was sounded five
hundred times for the souls of the dead. This bell was wrung
fifteen minutes after the community retired, in a dark eerie
corridor on the ground floor, said to be haunted by the ghost
of a mad nun who drowned herself.

Twenty minutes after the rest of the nuns went to bed, while
she was ringing the *De Profundis* bell, a sudden apparition on
the stairs so terrified Clair that she nearly dropped the bell.
She only just managed to muffle a scream before realizing
that it was Sister Mary Thomas, a first year novice, sliding
down the banister in a long white nightdress.

After lunch the following day, Clair was summoned to
Mother Virtue's office.

'Do you really want to be a nun, Clair?' she asked, seating
herself with a display of grandeur before the kneeling girl.

'Yes, reverend mother,' Clair answered with a heavy heart.
She had failed to report the incident of the previous night.

'This morning, one of your companions, with contrite
humility, admitted to a serious breach of the Holy Rule.'

Clair felt weighted to the floor.

'I have prayed, I have prayed, I have waited, I have waited,
I have hoped, hoped, hoped, Clair, that you would come to
me and humbly confess. But no, you are too proud. Too
lacking in humility. Do you think the Holy Rule does not

apply to you, sister?'

'No, mother,' Clair replied.

'Did you observe a sister in breach of the Holy Rule?'

After a moment's silence, Clair said feebly, 'Yes, mother.'

'Have you read the chapter of the Holy Rule which states the duty of a sister who finds one of her companions in breach of a rule?'

'No, mother,' Clair answered.

'And, why not, sister?'

'Because,' Clair answered, with a confidence that surprised herself then, 'as a lay person, I am not permitted to read the Holy Rule.'

This was the wrong answer. The worst possible answer. Mother Virtue rose.

'Your parents are very proud to have a daughter in a convent, are they not?' she asked, standing over the girl.

'Yes, they are.'

'Yes, indeed,' the superior repeated, turning with a grand sweeping movement towards her desk, 'a letter arrived from your father last week.'

The desk contained a large pile of letters. She picked up the wrong letter first. Discovering her mistake, she returned it to her desk. She picked up another letter. 'Yes,' she said, shaking it in Clair's direction, 'this is your father's letter. I shall read part of it to you now.'

"My dear Clair," she began,

> It was great to hear from you as usual and great to hear that you were doing well in the convent we got a letter from John he is doing well for himself in england he is working on a building site making good money he sends ten pounds home every week to his ma he is staying with an irish woman and she looks after him well he is always asking after you all the wains is doing well they are always asking after you as well I didn't tell you before but when you went away our wee Bernadette took it wile bad we had to get the priest to her thank God she is alright

now father Doherty was great he come up to talk to
her every day now she wants to be a nun too maybe
ill be lucky and have two daughters nuns God knows
that would be great youll never know how proud
your ma and me is of you pray for your brother in
england and pray for us all we are all looking forward
to seeing you on your big day august the fifteenth
father Doherty tells us it is a wile big do with the
bishop and all your ma has bought herself a new
hat and sent my suit to the cleaners...

She folded the letter, returned it to the desk and stood
again before the kneeling girl.

'How, Clair,' she said solemnly, 'would your parents feel if
you were dismissed as unsuitable?'

Clair was aghast.

'Humility,' Mother Virtue intoned, 'is the virtue most
pleasing to God. Practise humility and God will reward you.
God turns his back on no-one. Even your father. Yes, Clair,
we know all about the years he spent in prison. From your
own priest, Father Curry. But even your father is now a
reformed character. Your father has turned to God and the
Lord has rewarded him with a righteous and contrite heart.
You must do likewise. Now go to the chapel and pray to God
for this great gift. May God bless you child, and always keep
you in his sight.'

Clair kissed the floor and before rising, as was customary,
asked Mother Virtue for a blessing. When the woman placed
her hands on her shoulders, Clair felt a shudder run all the
way along her spine. On her way to the chapel, her thoughts
turned tenderly towards her home and her family. With a
sting of pain she tried to imagine her father sitting at a cluttered
corner of the table, with the din of the younger children ringing
in his ears, clutching an unfamiliar pen in his clumsy hand.
Her heart grew sick as she thought of him, struggling for words
to write to her, unaware that she would never read them.

A novice could normally expect to end her stay in the novitiate after seven years. Ten days before reception or profession, a sister was expected to withdraw from normal activities and move to one of the isolated cells in the most secluded part of the house known as the hermitage, to prepare herself, through solitary prayer and meditation, for the important step she was about to take.

Six senior novices were due to make final vows on the same day as Clair's reception, and to move on to work in schools and hospitals in Latin America. On the evening before the retreat commenced, Mother Virtue announced that only five of the six would be leaving to take up missionary duties. Sister Mary Philomena, a novice some ten years older than the others, was told that she must remain behind to take up the duties of assistant cook in the convent kitchen.

Two days before she was due to make her final profession, Sister Philomena left her isolated cell and went to the stairs that led to the upper floors. No-one saw her go. Several hours later, her body was found in a courtyard beneath an open window. The coroner's report stated that this woman, who seven years earlier had given up a promising career as a paediatrician, had taken her life while the balance of her mind had been disturbed.

Mother Virtue left the house on the day after the suicide. Some said she had been called to the mother house in Rome to give an account of the tragedy to the mother general. Others, that she had gone into hiding following threats from the dead nun's brothers. Some were even sure she had had a nervous breakdown. Rumour followed rumour for a number of months until the day she arrived back, from where nobody knew.

At first, she did not visit the novitiate, but spent hours kneeling motionlessly in the chapel, like some spectre from another world. Then with the approach of Christmas, she threw off her cloak of silence, and returning to the novitiate, plunged into the festivities with unexpected enthusiasm.

On Christmas Eve she gathered the novices and postulants together in the novitiate, and announced that she had an important message to communicate. 'If we are to live in a modern world, sisters, we must learn to move with the times,' she began in elevated tones. 'We must throw open a window on the world and allow the fresh winds of progress to blow away the cobwebs from our minds. Sisters, I give you the news that from now on you will all be permitted to use disposable sanitary towels. Isn't that wonderful, sisters.'

There was a general murmur of approval and some suppressed laughter disguised behind faked coughs and shuffling feet. Only Clair regarded her with angry silence. "We must throw open a window on the world," how could she choose those words after what happened to poor Sister Philomena.

'I can see we are not all agreed, Sister Mary Joseph,' the superior addressed Clair as a novice for the first time. 'Do you not think this news is wonderful?'

'No, mother. Not wonderful,' Clair answered. 'If violence, cruelty, greed, hunger and disease were wiped from the face of the earth, then Mother, I would describe that as wonderful,' Clair said.

Clair expected no normal reprimand or penance for this outspoken act of defiance. She expected to be sent home, but when Christmas and New Year passed without the expected summons to the office she started to suppose that Mother Virtue had really changed and had decided to forgive her. The superior visited the novitiate every day and behaved as if the incident had never happened. It was noticed too, that since her return, she had not handed down a single penance.

During the first week of February, when Clair's turn came to ring the bell, Mother Virtue paid an unexpectedly early visit to the novitiate. She was not her animated, exuberant self. 'Sisters,' she said gravely, 'I would like you all to follow me.' She led them from the room, down the stairs, along a corridor, and out through a seldom used door at the back of the building.

The baffled novices walked behind her in single file, till she halted them at the far corner of a garden. There they found Sister Mary Helen in a pair of waders, her habit hitched up around her waist, standing knee-deep in an open sewer, shovelling shit, sanitary towels and boxes of chocolates out onto the ground.

Explanations for Mary Helen's insanity circulated in whispers among the novices and postulants all morning. One of the two sisters from the Bogside said her insanity must have been hereditary because, looking at Mary Helen, you could tell right away that she wasn't all there. Others, that Mother Virtue had driven her mad. Sister Mary Hilda, a novice from Dublin believed to have had a university education, explained how a doctor named Freud could show that sexual perversion was directing Mary Helen when she dug all the shit out of the sewer and mixed it up with chocolates and sanitary towels.

At four o'clock that afternoon, Sister Mary Helen walked into the novitiate looking neat and clean in a fresh habit. Every eye in the room followed her. She walked up to Clair and ordered her to go to the office. Clair was perplexed. Was Mary Helen better? Should she go? After a moment's indecision, Clair decided to obey and walked down the corridor with Mary Helen on her heels.

When she got to the office she was met by Mother Virtue, Mother Peter, and Sister Veronica.

'What time did you get out of bed this morning, Sister Mary Joseph?' the reverend mother asked as the girl was sinking to her knees.

'At the usual time,' Clair answered, then remembering, corrected herself. 'No, I got up when the clock alarmed, and this morning, for some reason, it went off fifteen minutes early.'

'Did you set it to alarm early?' Mother Virtue asked.

'I am not permitted to set the alarm. That job is Sister Mary Helen's.'

'Did you set the clock to alarm at the usual time?' the superior asked, turning to Sister Mary Helen who was sitting with her head bowed awkwardly to hide a face crimson with embarrassment.

'Yes, mother,' Mary Helen muttered without raising her

head.

'You have heard Sister Mary Helen's reply. What have you got to say for yourself?', the reverend mother demanded.

'I can only repeat what I said before,' Clair answered, confused.

'If the alarm woke you too early, why did you not stay in bed?'

'Because I did not realize that it was too early. I put my hand out to stop it automatically. I probably did not open my eyes. It was four in the morning. When I became fully awake, I followed the rules precisely. I got out of bed, kissed the floor, made a morning offering, washed, dressed, stripped our bed, and checked the time.'

'Very well, sister, but would you mind telling us what you did then?' Mother Virtue asked and forced a smile.

'When I realized I had extra time, I went down to the novitiate.'

Mother Virtue clapped her hands and turned to the others triumphantly. 'She admits it, sisters,' she said. 'We have found our thief.'

'Admits what?', Clair asked, half rising. 'Did you call me a thief?'

'Yes, sister. You went to the novitiate this morning while the rest of the community was asleep, and stole boxes of chocolates from the cupboard.'

'I did not. I went to the novitiate to our drawer to get a peppermint to freshen our breath because I had no toothpaste. Sister Mary Helen can tell you that I asked her for permission to go to our suitcase yesterday to get a fresh tube as the one I had went missing...'

'Did this novice seek your permission to get toothpaste from our suitcase yesterday?'

'No, mother,' Mary Helen muttered.

Mother Virtue turned to Clair again. 'Are you accusing Sister Mary Helen of lying?', she demanded.

'No, mother,' Clair said, 'She may have forgotten.'

'Are you a forgetful person, Sister Mary Helen?', Mother

Virtue enquired playfully. Mary Helen, continuing to blush, replied 'No.'

'Sister Mary Helen has not forgotten. What do you have to say now?'

'I went to the novitiate to get one of our peppermints.'

'If that is the case, why did you remain there for two or three minutes? It wouldn't take that time to take a peppermint from our drawer,' Mother Virtue continued.

'I had to stay there long enough to eat the peppermint because it is forbidden for a sister to eat in any part of the house, save the refectory or the novitiate.'

'Well, well,' Mother Virtue addressed the other three nuns. 'Now she claims to be concerned with keeping the Holy Rule.'

'I am telling the truth, mother,' Clair exploded, 'and since entering this house, I have always done my best to keep the Holy Rule.'

'Do you hear that?', Mother Virtue shook her head. 'Now she is mocking God.'

Clair spoke in a quiet firm voice. 'The Holy Rule says that a sister is absolutely forbidden to leave her bed during the Great Silence. I was the *only* sister with permission to be out of bed before the awakening bell this morning. The Holy Rule was breached by the person who watched me go to the novitiate. If she had been less anxious to cover up her own fault, she would naturally have followed me into the room to find out what I was doing there. Who was that, reverend mother? Was it you?'

A bell, a bell that Clair should have been ringing, sounded in the corridor below. Everyone rose to go.

'Stay right where you are, Sister Mary Joseph,' the superior snapped as Clair bent down to kiss the floor. The other three women bowed and left.

When they were alone, Mother Virtue did not speak at first but paced slowly around the room, apparently deep in thought. When she broke the silence at last, Clair was almost disarmed by her friendliness. 'My dear sister,' she began, coming to a halt before Clair and placing a hand on each of her shoulders, 'you are here to serve God. Isn't that so?'

'Yes, mother,' Clair answered cautiously.

'And the best way to serve God is to obey your superiors. Isn't that so?'

'Yes, mother,' Clair answered again.

'Now, sister, you must listen while I read to you a passage from *The Imitation of Christ.* A passage on obedience.'

She went to the desk and picked up her copy:

> Everyone gladly does whatever he most likes; but if God is to dwell among us, we must sometimes yield our own opinions for the sake of peace.

She stopped to look at the kneeling girl before continuing:

> If your opinion is sound, and you forgo it for the love of God and follow that of another, *you will win great merit.* It may even come about that each of two opinions is good; but to refuse to come to agreement with others when reason or occasion demand it, *is a sign of pride and obstinacy.*

'Did you understand all that I read you my child?' she asked.

'Yes, mother,' Clair answered.

'You have already agreed that the best way to serve God is to obey your superiors in all things, isn't that so child?' she continued in the same friendly manner.

'It is, mother,' Clair agreed again.

'Then, sister, I'm sure you would like to be chosen to do something very special for God. Something that would bring blessings not only on you, but also on your parents, brothers and sisters.'

'Yes, mother, I would,' Clair answered.

'Good,' the superior smiled warmly. 'You are learning true humility. At last you are coming to realize that only the Christ-fettered are free.'

She placed an affectionate arm round the girl's shoulder. 'Here is what I want you to do sister,' she said, looking earnestly into Clair's eyes. 'When the bell rings for supper this evening,

I want you to go to the centre of the refectory, and bearing in mind the words of Thomas a Kempis I want you to confess to the community that you took boxes of chocolates from the novitiate this morning, and that you later panicked and flushed them down the toilet. In this way, dear sister, you will gain great merit.'

Clair was stunned almost to the point of paralysis. When she could speak again, her voice appeared to be coming from a place far outside herself. 'I cannot do that. You are asking me to bear false witness.'

'I have been mistaken,' Mother Virtue snapped, 'You have not yet learned humility. Kneel down at once. You are vain and full of self.'

Weary, confused and on the verge of tears, Clair knelt down. Again Mother Virtue paced the room. Again she returned to stand over Clair. 'I will give you one last chance,' she said. 'If you obey, the whole matter will be forgotten. If you do not, tomorrow I will call in a friend of mine, a senior detective. You will be arrested and charged with theft. Your name will be in all the papers. Your family will be in disgrace.'

'So be it,' Clair answered, a cold anger taking possession of her. 'I have nothing to fear. I will get a fair hearing in a court. I have nothing to fear from newspapers either. They'd love to hear all about you. Call whoever you like, I will not be bullied, I will not lie.'

'You will not serve God. That is quite clear,' the reverend mother shrieked. 'The devil is the one you serve.'

'I serve God,' Clair corrected, 'The God whose greatest gift is free will. But I will not serve your God.'

'You are possessed by the devil. Satan has given you the gift of tongues,' the superior spat.

Clair could not stop herself. 'Look what you have done to Sister Mary Helen. Your lying has driven her mad.'

'Get out of here, you devil. Get out at once,' Mother Virtue screamed, hurling herself at Clair and kicking her several times before she managed to struggle to her feet.

Clair stumbled out of the office in tears. She had no idea what to do or who to turn to. It was already dark outside and Athgar was two miles away. She was not even sure in which direction. She decided to walk to the nearest farmhouse and ask to use a telephone. Ring Father Doherty. He would tell her what to do. She looked with uncertainty at her habit. She was not sure whether she should wear it or not. She decided she would. It would only make matters worse for her if she went to the storeroom to change without permission.

She made her way quickly to the ground floor and along the corridor leading to the outside door. It was securely locked and bolted. Hearing footsteps approach she turned around and saw Mother Peter hurrying towards her. The novice mistress embraced her and offered her the kiss of peace. Clair broke down and sobbed loudly. 'What is going on, mother? Why did Mother Virtue try so hard to make me lie?'

Mother Peter led Clair into a doorway before replying. 'Please do not think of the events of today again, sister,' she said softly, 'As you know, the Lord acts in strange and mysterious ways. It is not for us to question his ways, but to accept them. We must all carry the cross he has laid down for us. If your cross is a heavy one, sister, that is merely a reflection of how deeply he loves you. He is testing your vocation. Let us go to the chapel and pray for a moment in silence. Then I will take you to the refectory and find you some supper.'

Clair did not sleep that night or for several nights after. Regardless of how hard she tried to quell them, questions kept churning around in her mind. Questions that she could at first find no reasonable answers for. Was it possible that Sister Mary Helen was mad, after all? And if so, could she have cooked the whole thing up and managed to convince Mother Virtue? It was possible. She was certainly responsible for the clock. But that did not account for Mother Virtue's behaviour. Mother Virtue was not mad. Mother Virtue was something entirely different. That woman had, for some reason, tried to set her up and had not quite succeeded. If that was the case, would she try again? And what was Mother

Peter's role in all this?

But as the days that followed passed quietly and stretched into weeks without further incident, Clair's mind began to settle and her sleep returned. It was then, for the first time, that she thought of Mother Peter's words of comfort that night in the corridor: "The Lord acts in strange and mysterious ways".

She wondered why she had not thought of them earlier. It was so simple. Everything became clear to her. God was testing her vocation. In the light of this new understanding, Mother Virtue's behaviour became explicable. During the interrogation she had been acting the part of devil's advocate. Other novices were probably put through similar tests. Maybe even the same one.

Following this revelation, Clair felt guilty for having misjudged the reverend mother and, satisfied that the matter was finally closed, she dismissed it from her mind and settled back into her normal routine.

On Tuesday evening eight weeks later when the novices were at choir practice, Sister Mary Helen came to Clair again and whispered, 'Follow me, sister.' Clair obeyed and was led down a strange corridor to a part of the house she had never been to before. She was ushered into a room that was unfurnished, save for a table. On top of it sat Clair's suitcase. A door opposite the one she entered, opened off the room on to a pathway that led to the drive.

Mother Virtue entered.

'Take off your habit and put on your secular clothes,' she ordered. 'Then leave by that door. Your father is waiting.'

Clair obeyed. She didn't resist. She didn't want to. It was over. She changed back into her clothes. They no longer fitted. When she started to fold her habit, the thin voice addressed her once more. 'Take your hands off the holy habit, you have defiled it for the last time.'

Looking into Mother Virtue's eyes, Clair was violently confronted for the first time with her own folly and innocence. Burning with anguish and anger she turned to walk away.

'Just one moment,' called the reverend mother, drawing an envelope from the slit at the side of her habit and holding it out to her.

'Your money is in this envelope. Check it before you leave.'

Clair took the envelope and opened it. Inside she found a crumpled five pound note, the rent money her mother had given the nuns more than two years before. She clutched it to her and walked out into the light.